AISLE 5

AISLE 5

CAT AUSTEN

Cat Austen

This is a work of fiction. Names, characters, businesses, places, events, locales, and incidents are either the products of the author's imagination or used in a fictitious manner. Any resemblance to actual persons, living or dead, or actual events is purely coincidental.

Copyright © 2022 Cat Austen
All rights reserved. This book or parts thereof may not be reproduced in any form, stored in any retrieval system, or transmitted in any form by any means—electronic, mechanical, photocopy, recording, or otherwise—without prior written permission of the author, except as provided by United States of America copyright law. Quotes used for review purposes are cool, though.

ISBN: 979-8-9893873-0-4

Cover design by K.B. Barrett Designs

Self-published by the author because she's a control freak.

www.catausten.com

Titles by Cat Austen

Convergence- *August 2022*- a polyamorous, contemporary, romantic suspense.

Aisle 5- *November 2022*- a contemporary, erotic, romantic comedy.

Solace- *Aug 2023*- book one in a mafia why choose trilogy. Dark romcom.

Spite- *November 2023*- book two in the Solace series.

Check out catausten.com, subscribe to newsletter, and follow on amazon.com for all new releases.

This book is dedicated to stay-at-home moms who use spicy books as their escape. If you sometimes feel like you're not *you* anymore- you're just Mom- know that I see *you* and I love you. Writing is how I found *me* again and it started with reading.

This book was written after bedtime amongst the mess of each day.

This book is also dedicated to the pumpkin spice latte, Ugg wearing, Gilmore Girl watching, basic bitches who are freaks in the bedroom.

Author's Note

This book is not for anyone under the age of 18. While this is a cozy romantic comedy, it *also* contains scenes of explicit sexual content including knife play, blood play, rope restraint, condomless sex, dirty talk, voyeurism, and exhibitionism. If you are under 18 and your mom catches you reading this, you can't say I didn't warn you.

This book is not meant to be a guide to BDSM in any way. Please do your own research so you can be kinky safely. Leave the unsafe practices to the fictional characters.

If you are triggered by any of this content, please call your therapist.

If you think you know me in real life, turn away now. Please, my brother in Christ, I'm begging you.

I

Sixty-seven...

The left eye of the college's dean of curriculum sleepily drooped closed to join the right as slumber finally claimed him. He had put up a valiant fight, but alas, the May morning sun and ambient white noise of microphone static proved too potent of a nap inducing drug for the octogenarian. I jerked upright in my seat in silent celebration and looked at the other graduates next to me on the school's genetically modified green front lawn. I was hoping to grab the attention of someone else who had witnessed Mr. Collins succumb to a cozy, little afternoon nap on stage. But the unseasonably balmy morning was getting to everyone. The surrounding graduates lounged in their metal folding lawn chairs. Some fidgeted with tassels or the copy paper program of events, some outright slept, and some were covertly on their phones.

Sixty-six...

I sighed quietly and returned to my position of watching my professors and the other esteemed leaders I had never seen before, preside over the graduation of my community college. I was graduating with my Associate of Arts degree in business and was impatient to leave. While this degree was something I had worked towards and was proud of, this wasn't the end for me. This was just another box to tick along the way to owning my bookstore and café. This wasn't even the last thing I had to do today, and I had just over an hour until my shift at work started.

Sixty-five minutes...

Mr. Collins twitched in his sleep and elbowed the stack of embossed pleather diplomas. Two slid off the top, landing with a *plop* that startled anyone not paying attention. A professor scrambled to get them back into the correct order, and the scuffle was enough to shake the local businessman, who was currently discussing the merits of the business program from which I was just about to graduate. He ended his speech quickly and the calling of the names began directly after. The tidy rows of graduates became more alert as the main event approached.

Fifty-two minutes...

I discreetly checked my watch as I reclaimed my space with the other A surnames on the folding lawn chair after walking across the stage, shaking hands with the leaders of the college, and accepting my diploma. The surrounding people were quietly discussing their plans after graduation, ranging from going home to families to going to parties, and I only felt bad for myself for a second. I could have easily not worked today, but there was no way I would miss the well-planned event at work.

Forty-one...

The last group of graduates of my small school walked across the stage and accepted their diplomas, and a relieved applause followed the last name called. The professor that had called out every name had a pink blush to her cheeks and eagerly accepted a bottle of water. I sat up and looked at the ground around my seat as if I had carried anything onto the lawn with me other than my car key that was safely stowed in my left bra cup. I readied to stand but someone else came up to the podium and the crowd seemed to groan and sigh without actually groaning and sighing.

Twelve...

I panted as I slammed my car door behind me and started the engine. I had sprinted to my car and was peeling out of there as fast as I could to beat the meandering crowds. While being late to work on the day that I graduated college would have been excusable with my perfect history, I still wanted to keep my track record of being dependable.

Eleven minutes late...

Oscar had a twelve-minute rule for tardiness, and I was testing it as I blew through the staff entrance of Oscar's grocery store and clocked in at six seconds before I was twelve minutes late. A cacophony accompanied my wild and sprinting entrance. The metal door slammed against the cement wall, someone shouted in alarm, a chair scraped back, and a coffee mug hit the tile floor.

"Damn it, Layla!" Donna's rasping smoker's voice sounded as

I raised my hands over my head in triumph and clutched my clock in slip.

"I told you to get here when you could," Oscar said in a shocked voice.

"And I could," I said breathlessly and walked to my assigned locker.

"Did you run off the stage and come straight here?" Donna asked with a wheezing laugh. She threw paper towels on the floor to soak up her coffee.

I looked down at my solid blue sack of a gown that I still wore, and my tassel slid down before my eyes. I opened my locker and balled my cap and gown onto the shelf. "Basically," I laughed. I had worn my costume under my graduation gown, and just needed to put my brunette hair into little space buns to complete my look for May the Fourth Star Wars and Cinco de Mayo Week. I was costumed as Princess Leia for the cumulative Cinco de Mayo cookout this evening. Oscar loved a good dual-purpose celebration. And tacos and Star Wars brought in a crowd.

"Well, I think this deserves a celebratory toast, don't you, Oscar?" Donna asked. Her cheerful scrape of a voice only meant trouble for Oscar, and I grinned as I pinned my last space bun.

Oscar, who had retreated to his little back of the house office, leaned to see us in his creaking office chair. "What's that?" he asked suspiciously, having noted her tone before her words. His bushy mustache seemed to pucker as his lips bunched.

"Oscar, mark out a few bottles of champagne for Layla," Donna called to him as she hurried out the swinging staff door to the store. The sound of the Star Wars soundtracks that played on repeat all week snuck in the door in bursts as it swung behind Donna.

"Champagne?" Oscar asked warily as he hefted his round stomach out of his seat and came out of his office.

Donna returned with three bottles of prosecco, and Oscar sputtered in protest. His bushy gray mustache bounced and sweat beaded on his forehead. "Donna," he scolded, but it came out as a squeak.

"Alright, fine, one bottle," Donna said with a dramatic roll of her eyes before winking covertly at me.

I giggled and Oscar shuffled back to his office, seemingly not willing to fight with Donna today. Donna was likely to walk out, and she was the only one willing to wear the Yoda costume.

After a few glasses of champagne quickly drank before Oscar came to his senses, and a giggle fit at Donna's costume, we were on the floor and working.

James, a local high school student who worked afternoons, was dressed as Luke Skywalker, seeing as he was the only male on the store's staff that fit into the men's medium sized costume that was purchased for a long past employee. James, as Luke, was greeting customers as they entered while his girlfriend, dressed as a Storm Trooper, kept groping Luke rather than trying to kill him. Chewbacca was actually one of Oscar's corgis, wearing a fuzzy hooded costume on a leash at James' side and happily licking a plush Millennium Falcon.

A deep chuckle caught my attention while I worked in check out. I looked up to see Han Solo, or rather my manager, Benjamin, approaching his station in the next lane. It was close to the afternoon rush, so a second lane would open, and a manager had to be up front. Thus, my near frantic ringing could slow to a more regular speed. Benjamin laughed again, a deep, almost sexy sound. I knew the laugh was fake, though. Last year there had been a snafu with the catering at the Christmas party and Donna had been left in charge of the last-minute planning and she had mistaken Edible Arrangements, the place that made fruit bouquets, with Edible Entertainment, a company that provided topless cocktail waitresses. We had ended up with an odd company party with all twenty employees, two delivery drivers, and about seven topless cocktail waitresses. Everyone had laughed hysterically for hours, including the beautiful waitresses and Benjamin. Benjamin, who was generally a jovial person with an easy laugh, had been so tickled that his genuine laugh kicked through the practiced one. His actual laugh was a lilting, high pitched, infectious sound.

Benjamin plopped onto his stool at his lane and opened up his register, still chatting with the young boy of a mom who was heavy with a second pregnancy. She smiled as she stacked her purchases on the belt and her son continued his lisping recount of a Star Wars game he had played. Benjamin's short, curly blonde hair wasn't reminiscent of Han Solo at all, but the child still believed the costume.

I finished ringing out a harried man who was purchasing all the necessary "wife is mad at me" items. As he hurried out the door, I smiled and gave him a "good luck." I was a quick and efficient employee and was an expert at bagging groceries as I rang them. I had worked for Oscar at this store, Allen Family Groceries (affectionately called "Oscar's") since I was fifteen and had just celebrated my ten-year work anniversary. Though, it was nothing on Donna, who had worked here when Oscar's dad owned the place thirty years ago.

Benjamin had worked here for five years now, and he was by far the slowest ringer. Not by ability, but because he chatted with everyone that came through. He bought candy or fruit to give to children that came through his line. And when flowers were near expiration, he would mark out bouquets and hand blooms to every woman. I had tried the candy bit once and started a child's tantrum in check out. I left that level of customer service to the tall, fit, and attractive Benjamin.

Despite his slower pace, his line was intentionally longer than mine. It didn't bother me until a regular customer brought it up that afternoon.

"Well, it looks to me like the customers are playing favorites," chuckled Greg, of next door's Greg's Pharmacy.

I punched the keys on my register and provided him with his change. "Yeah, well, I can't wink to win them over," I laughed.

Benjamin spun on his stool to face me with a sly grin. "Really?"

I shrugged. "I end up closing both eyes."

"Show me," Benjamin demanded. Greg was slow to pocket his change and Benjamin's current customer waited with a smile.

"No," I said with mock seriousness.

"Hm," Benjamin said, considering me. "Then I guess we'll have a competition."

"Oh?" I said as I started ringing the next customer, who was watching us like it was a delightful TV drama.

"Yes, whoever gets through the most customers in the next hour wins. If I win, you'll wink at me every day for a week, with witnesses. And if you win, I'll do your closing duties for a week," Benjamin challenged me.

Our little audience chuckled.

"You're on," I accepted, and we leaned over our workspaces to shake on it.

Benjamin set a timer on his phone and started it. We were both considerably quieter while we worked now. The first few customers had been in on the challenge and were the most well behaved, orderly, and timely customers I had ever seen in my grocery store career. After that, all bets were off for how the customers behaved. I accomplished two returns, which required Benjamin's managerial approval, a raincheck for organic strawberries, and a grand total of fourteen customers served.

Benjamin handed me his register print out that tallied his sales for a set time period as he moved around my stool to check my numbers. He was sweating slightly; a sheen was visible on his forehead and in the deep V-neck of his costume. I breathed deeply, allowing myself five seconds of crushing on my manager dressed like a sweaty, tattooed Han Solo. He smelled like Old Spice deodorant, sweat, and dusty cotton.

Benjamin gave a small gasp and looked down at me. I looked over the printout he had handed me and located his number: twelve.

"Did I win?" I asked and wiped a bead of my sweat off my forehead and tried to look over his shoulder.

"You did," he groaned in defeat.

I gave an "Aha!" of triumph and danced in my workspace.

"Alright, alright," he harrumphed and returned to his space with a dramatic pout.

My mood remained high for the rest of my shift, which included extra time at the Cinco de Mayo cookout. Darth Vader (Oscar) made shrimp and black bean tacos and I devoured more than one of each. When Benjamin finished my closing duties, he dramatically fell into a seat at the table where only staff remained under the twinkling lights strung up over the front of the store. He had removed the vest of his Han Solo costume and was now only wearing the loose beige shirt with the deep V-neck. He looked devastating with his tattoos peeking out at his hands and neck. I swallowed the last of my soda and tried to avert my gaze, looking instead at Donna, who was openly staring at Benjamin.

"You know, if you ever get tired of working here, those girls over at Edible Entertainment would hire you to be a topless waiter in a second," Donna called to him in her rasping voice. Benjamin was only a year older than me, and much younger than married Donna, so everyone knew she was teasing him.

"Okay, that- that's... harassment," Benjamin said in a sharp, disappointed tone, but his grin and deep blush showed he wasn't actually angry. He picked up the remaining plate of tacos and went back into the store to eat alone. The remaining staff laughed good-naturedly and called him back.

It was late now, well past closing, and I was exhausted. I was yawning widely by the time we had finished cleaning up the cookout and were all heading towards our cars. I sat in silence in my car for a moment before I could muster the strength to drive home. Donna waited in her car for me to drive off, always the protective mother type, so I felt motivated enough to drive out of the lot.

I checked the mail at the front door of my apartment building before shuffling down to my favorite place in the world. I had created a space so full of books and cozy places to read that I often found it difficult to leave. And some days I only left to get that feeling of coming home again. The feeling that a warm drink, a cozy robe, and a brilliant book was waiting for me.

2

My next shift at work was Sunday morning. It was sunny and warm already, but still quiet on the historical street Oscar's store inhabited. Greg's pharmacy was open, and I could hear saxophone music from the sidewalk. On the other side of Oscar's was a furniture store owned by the Schmidts who were so often on vacations that I never knew if the store was open. Our town worked hard to maintain the historical charm of this street. The brick storefronts all had hanging flowers and lights and clean windows. Donna was out front smoking and watering our flowers when I crossed the small cobblestone street from the main parking lot. The most modern feature added to the street were the crosswalks from the storefronts to a clean parking lot across the street. The second most modern feature was the now vintage Coke machine outside the store that was there for the aesthetic, as it hadn't worked in fifteen years.

"Mornin' peaches," Donna greeted me with her cigarette hanging from her lips.

"Morning, Donna," I replied happily and stopped to smell the begonias. There wasn't much of a scent, but it seemed like the right thing to do. "These look lovely."

"Eh, they're boring. Oh, Oscar asked to see you." Donna shrugged.

I made my way to the staff room, bypassing a few morning shoppers. I was vaguely worried about the meeting, knowing I had done nothing wrong. I stopped first at my locker to leave my purse and grab my apron and name tag before clocking in.

"Layla! Good morning! Can you come here for a minute?" Oscar called.

He was in his seat at the massive antique wooden desk. His chair was new, as he often broke them by plopping down on the seat. I perched on the edge of the old pharmacy waiting room chair (courtesy of a remodel Greg did ten years ago) across from his desk and straightened my apron.

"Here, have some breakfast," Oscar said. He pulled out a lunchbox and took out a tomato sauce-stained Tupperware with eggs and bacon in it. It was still hot. He slid it across the desk to me and then pulled out a heavily buttered croissant and slid it next to the container.

"Um, I already ate. Oscar, is this *your* breakfast? Are you firing me?" I asked, sitting up ramrod straight in the chair.

He startled like I had scared him and fumbled with the silverware he had clearly brought from home and not out of the staff kitchenette. "What?! No!"

My heart sank to my stomach. "Who died?" I whispered.

Oscar sputtered nervously and his mustache quivered but waved a hand dismissively to say nobody had died. I relaxed minutely. He gathered himself and gestured for me to eat. I knew

Oscar was a great cook, so I took a few bites in silence while Oscar gathered himself to speak.

"Are you leaving us, Layla?" he asked quietly.

"No? What makes you think that?" I asked and swallowed my bite of delicious eggs.

"You've just graduated and I- I'm sure you have... grander plans than working here forever," Oscar explained.

"I love working here," I said a bit more forcefully than needed. I set down my utensils. "Oscar, I'm not leaving. At least, not right now. Do I have plans to leave? Sort of. A lot has to happen first."

"What are those plans, if I may ask?" He was genuine in his concern.

I would have never answered any other boss, but Oscar was basically family. "I want to own a bookstore with a café."

Oscar's eyes lit up and his mustache jumped. "Oh, that's wonderful, Layla!"

"I have a lot more time here before I make any changes. I don't exactly have the capital needed to buy a store," I said and leaned back in my chair now that I knew I wasn't being fired.

"I want to support you and your dreams," Oscar said after a thoughtful moment. He spun in his chair to a filing cabinet behind him. He rummaged for a moment before turning back. "I might have an opportunity for you. You see, maybe six months ago that big chain store across town started offering twenty-four-hour service. I did a bit of polling and checked out what their sales were like in the overnight hours, and I think we should give it a go."

Oscar loathed twenty-four-hour stores. This was a big step.

"I was thinking of maybe just the summer to start. As a trial, you see," Oscar continued. "If you all felt you wanted to, that is."

"So, like, double shifts?" I asked. I wasn't completely opposed to it. I was often up reading most of the night, anyway.

"No, rotating overnight shifts," Oscar corrected. Then rushed to say, "With a pay increase!"

I hummed in consideration. "How much of a raise?"

It was clear Oscar hadn't thought this far into the plan. "An extra... three dollars an hour."

"Hmm, that's only twenty-four dollars more a shift," I said discernibly.

"An extra thirty dollars a shift, whatever the math is," Oscar said quickly.

We stared at each other with narrowed eyes for a moment before he realized I was needling him. He huffed in realization and his mustache ruffled.

"When would this start?" I asked with a smile.

"After... our coloring contest and cereal testing party next week," he planned as he spoke.

"Well, I'm in," I said happily.

A chime sounded on Oscar's laptop, and he hurried to pull up a camera feed of his corgis. He had three at home, and he trained them to press a button that video called Oscar while he was away. These dogs were his pride and joy and the only things keeping him going after the death of his late wife. He had a daughter that he loved dearly who was married and had two little girls, but his corgis were his babies.

I left the office while Oscar cooed at his dogs and went up front to where Donna was waiting for the gossip. I filled her in before I opened up my register. She was next to my lane organizing the printouts of a cartoon version of our store and a grocery cart for the coloring contest. Everyone knew Donna. She had worked at Oscar's forever. She and her husband ran the corgi rescue Oscar adopted from, and they basically lived at the local bar, Scoot's. Donna talked to all of my customers as they came through my line and ended up taking over ringing people out and I made my way to work on inventory.

When working inventory, we could wear headphones, and I loved a great audiobook. I was well into a fantastic novel, slowly shelving cans when Benjamin was next to me and tapped my shoulder. My heart leapt, not expecting someone to be so close, and ended up smacking his hand away with a can of beans.

"Woah," Benjamin tried to soothe me like I was a spooked horse.

"Sorry!" I said and ripped my earbuds out with my bean-free hand.

"It's alright," he chuckled. "Though I hope you don't always startle so aggressively."

A customer murmured an "Excuse me," and Benjamin stepped closer to me so she could push her cart past us. He didn't step back after she was through. Instead, he picked up my hand that was still clutching the can of beans and gently took the can out of my hand.

"D-do you plan on startling me more often?" I stammered, confused. I was acutely aware of the sweat forming on my forehead.

"No, we're being paired up for the overnight shift," he

explained in a quiet voice. One corner of his lips lifted in almost a smirk. His brown eyes were kind and focused on mine.

"Oh!" I exclaimed. My throat went dry.

"Yeah, it'll be... fun," he drawled. I saw the hint of a blush forming at his neck. His tattoos hid it well, but he had a ferocious blush.

"Fun," I echoed, but my voice was a squeak with how dry my throat was.

"I just hope you're not scared of the dark or something," he teased. He picked up my hand again and placed the can of beans back in my palm before backing away.

"Oh, no. I'm great in the dark," I tried to reassure him in my strange, dry voice. I realized the innuendo after I finished saying it and my blush became almost as prominent as his.

"Great," he said, still backing away. His rosiness was very apparent as it crept over his cheeks. He was so fair skinned it appeared in almost blotches. He ran a hand through the curly blonde hair that he kept longer on top and gave a full smirk. "So am I."

And with that he left me speechless, sweaty, parched, and still clutching a can of green beans. I took a water break before returning to my post in the canned goods aisle. What was Oscar thinking, pairing me up with Benjamin for overnights? Not that we didn't get along. That wasn't the case. But wouldn't Oscar think I was better paired with Donna? Though she would never work overnight. She and her husband had to make sure Scoot's bar wasn't empty. James? He was a minor and there were probably laws against him working overnight. There were twenty employees at this store, and he chose Benjamin?

I tried listening to my audiobook again but kept getting lost in my own thoughts and having to rewind. Eventually, I gave up and switched it off. Working with Benjamin for five years before working overnight together should have been a simple transition. Though, we had never been alone together other than occasional breaks in the staff room. All of our conversations had been about work. It had been a very professional relationship- a positive one, but professional. We were close in age, but we weren't friends.

Donna and I had lunch together at the picnic table outside the store. She smoked and drank a heavily sweetened iced tea while I picked at my sandwich.

"Not hungry?" Donna asked and took a long drag of her second cigarette of our break.

I opened my mouth to speak when the doors of the store swung out and the bell chimed cheerfully. I looked up to see Benjamin coming out, a can of soda in hand.

"Afternoon, ladies," he said and plopped down next to me on the bench and cracked open his soda. I bounced slightly on the bench as the wooden seat reacted to his weight.

I sat up straight and tidied my area. Donna smirked at me. I avoided all eye contact and hid the bite I had taken out of my sandwich. I had always been oddly self-conscious that one day someone would say I take big bites. Or small bites. I had yet to confirm that I took appropriately medium-sized bites of sandwiches.

"You hear the news, Donna?" Benjamin asked after chugging down his soda and stifling a belch. Even that did not dissuade my crush. "Layla and I are going to be overnight buddies."

"The both of you?" Donna cackled and ended with a wheezing cough.

"Yeah, Oscar has us paired up," Benjamin replied.

"Are you doing any overnights?" I asked, trying to divert attention.

"Hell no! I'm not giving Oscar any more of my time," Donna said and stamped out her cigarette. "But you two?" She cackled again.

I gathered my trash and got up abruptly. I didn't look at either of them. If Donna was about to allude to what I thought she was going to allude to, it would make working with Benjamin more awkward than it needed to be. "My lunch is over. See you both later!" I hurried back inside, where Oscar directed me to take over my register again.

Our store had busy times and slow times, but we were in a small town. Was there really a need to be open twenty-four hours? Maybe I could spend the time reading. Would he want to chat while we were stuck together? What would I talk to him about? All I knew about him was that he had tattoos, occasionally rode a motorcycle, and lived on the other side of town from my apartment. Who was I kidding? I also knew he wore Old Spice, was the only reason we had to order extra-large gloves, and made my stomach leap every time I saw him.

3

The day of the first overnight shift was also the day of our coloring contest and cereal tasting. Oscar knew how to throw a party and turned the occasion into a proper event. I was returning a few books to our local library before my shift and drove by and saw some of the action.

Children were squealing and running around. Someone was wearing a cow costume and holding jugs of milk, and there were streamers and balloons everywhere. I felt a little sad I wasn't involved, but excited to have a quiet shift at work. And excited to see Benjamin.

I was browsing the new books at the little lighthouse library when my phone buzzed in my pocket. It was Benjamin. He had texted me only once before about switching shifts with someone. This text was asking what coffee I liked from Beans & Leaves, a local coffee and tea shop. I texted back that I loved their London Fog tea latte with vanilla and thanked him. My stomach flipped at the idea of him ordering me a tea. Hurrying, I checked out at the library's circulation desk and got back down Main Street to Oscar's in record time.

Benjamin was exiting his rusty Honda just as I was pulling in. He grinned at me and bent back into his car. I almost hit Oscar's car as Benjamin's back distracted me in a thin t-shirt with a space between his waistband and shirt as he bent over. I parked somewhat sloppily and got out to meet him with a smile.

We could wear t-shirts and jeans rather than our usual polos and khakis for the overnight shift- a little perk Oscar came up with to make the job more appealing. I had cared little when he told us. What I wore didn't take away from the fact that I'd be working through the night. But now, seeing Benjamin's tattooed biceps in a dark gray t-shirt and his thighs filling out a pair of worn jeans, I could have kissed Oscar right on the mustache.

I approached Benjamin in my high-rise jeans and blue t-shirt that hugged my curves. He looked me over as he handed me my tea. "I don't know why, but I expected you to still be wearing the uniform," he said with a chuckle.

"Oscar didn't make you cover up your tattoos?" I asked in return. I looked up at him over the rim of my tea as I took a sip. The evening sun shone in my eyes, and I squinted through my smile.

Benjamin looked down at me for a moment, an expression I couldn't decipher in his eyes. He shook his head in reply and turned back to his car and pulled out his own coffee before slamming his door shut. "Let's do this," he said with a sigh before leading the way to the store. I thanked him for buying me a latte while we clocked in, and he elbowed me in response.

Oscar was waiting for us at the front of the store by the manager-on-duty office. He was clearly nervous and buzzing with energy. The clean-up from the cereal party was nearly finished, as two of our younger staff members swept and mopped the area.

"There you two are," he said excitedly, his mustache practically vibrating.

"Hey, Oscar," we chorused.

"I see you're both fueled up and ready," he chuckled and gestured to our drinks. "I don't think I'll sleep a wink and I haven't had coffee since this morning!"

"Oscar! You had two Diet Cokes before the cereal party!" Donna's voice rasped from her register. She pulled off her apron. "If they're here, can I go?"

Oscar waved her off with an annoyed expression. "Anyway, like we discussed before, have one register open, minimal cash in the drawer, and focus on doing the cleaning tasks we can't do during the day. Benjamin, I've left the ordering for you. Please stay in the front office for it. Don't leave Layla alone up front."

"Yes, sir," Benjamin said and sipped his coffee.

"Call me if you need anything," Oscar said, and I swear his mustache drooped.

"We won't need anything," Benjamin assured him calmly.

"But, if there's an emergency-" Oscar started.

"We know the number for 911," I said and ushered Oscar to his office.

"I have a security team coming to install cameras next week," Oscar said as he grabbed his lunchbox and laptop bag.

"That's so lovely. I feel so safe working here," I said and pushed him towards the doors to where we parked out back.

"If you want me to stay..."

"Goodbye, Oscar. Tell the babies we said hi and give them lots of belly rubs," Benjamin said and opened the back door.

Oscar's mustache bunched and trembled before he sighed and left us with a wave over his shoulder.

Benjamin looked at me with a roll of his eyes and a chuckle, and I mirrored his laugh. "He's so nervous. I bet he calls us throughout the night."

"I bet he calls four times," Benjamin said as we entered the store through the swinging staff doors.

"Hm, two calls and five texts," I countered.

"What's the stakes?" Benjamin asked me with a smirk.

"Whoever loses buys coffee next shift," I said with my own smile.

"Deal," he agreed, and we shook on it. As I shook his elaborately tattooed hand, I hoped my hand wasn't too clammy or dry. I had never paid much attention to what his tattoos were. I was afraid if I stared too long he'd think I was being a creep. But his right hand had the letters spelling out "hold" over his knuckles.

It was only a few minutes into our shift, after the usual closing shift left, when Benjamin stomped to the front door. He pushed it open forcefully and stood with his hands on his trim hips. "OSCAR!" he shouted. Oscar was in his car with his dogs, across the street in the parking lot. "GO HOME!"

Even from across the street, I could see Oscar's mustache moving before he turned his headlights off as if we'd not see him still there.

"OSCAR!" Benjamin shouted again.

I laughed from where I was working. Oscar turned his lights back on and left the parking lot with a conceding wave. Once he was gone, Benjamin came back in and was laughing his deep, practiced laugh.

There were a few people who came into the store in the later part of the evening after the store's typical closing hours. It remained a quiet evening until it had been a solid hour since the last customer. Benjamin and I both stayed near the front of the store, he with the ordering and office work, and I with wiping down the register belts and cleaning the impulse racks under the gum and candy. I moved to the produce section next.

Even though I had prepared for my overnight shift by napping in the late afternoon and having some caffeine, the darkness outside, quietness of the store, and cathartic cleaning of the produce section were relaxing me to want to go to sleep.

Benjamin came over to the produce section where I was working and leaned up against the cold case with a loud, wide yawn. I stifled my own sympathetic yawn. As he leaned back, his t-shirt rested against his abs and my eyes were stuck there until he spoke. I had to focus intently on cleaning the apple crates in order to function.

"That espresso was not enough," he said with a shake of his head.

"I'm so tired I could have been sleep cleaning before you came over," I said with a laugh. "Honestly, I don't remember cleaning the banana crate, but I know I did."

"I'm telling Oscar you were asleep on the job," Benjamin teased.

"Don't!" I whined with a laugh. "I truly don't know if he would take me off nights or set me up with a cot next to the register."

"He has called the store twice now," Benjamin said and rifled through the lettuce and made sure it was all fresh.

"I heard," I sighed. "It could go either way now."

"My coffee order is a dark chocolate mocha with an extra shot of espresso," he said confidently, and then licked his lips. "With a caramel drizzle."

I was struck with an intense wave of lust when he licked his lips. I was literally a perv. He was talking about coffee. He was talking about coffee. He was talking about coffee.

"That sounds sweet," I said, delayed.

"I have a monstrous sweet tooth," he said wistfully, looking into the middle distance.

"I would never know looking at you," I said without thinking. He truly had the body of a fictional man I would read about. The tattoos and muscles give very much Mafia Romance Hero. Morally Grey. Only Soft For Her vibes. But Benjamin was most definitely the opposite.

"I work out six days a week," he said, still dreamily. "Have you had Donna's peanut butter bars?"

"Of course," I replied, thinking of the tray of signature desserts she brought in for every birthday or party. They were so good we sometimes made up parties just so she would bake for us.

"One time, she had spilled her cigarette ashes over the top of part of the dish. I said I would throw that part out, but I sat in Oscar's office and ate it. Ashes and all. I am an actual animal for her peanut butter bars," Benjamin revealed.

"I mean, that's kind of gross, but I understand." I nodded solemnly.

He smiled a full smile at me. Benjamin's phone buzzed in

his pocket. He slid it out and laughed, looking at the message. He typed something back. "I think you're going to win the bet. Again."

"I thought I could feel Oscar's mustache moving from here," I said nonchalantly and continued my cleaning.

He looked at me in shock for a second.

"It's anthropomorphic," I explained and looked at him seriously.

Benjamin tipped his head back and let out a laugh. It was his genuine laugh. It was a silly, infectious sound and I couldn't help but join in. I wanted to hear this laugh every day. It was perfect.

"I always thought it was like his mood ring," Benjamin said when he calmed down enough to speak. "Sometimes I can tell what he's thinking just based on his mustache movement."

"Do you think it has its own independent thought?" I asked him with a giggle.

"Actually, yeah," he chuckled.

"See? Anthropomorphic."

"I haven't heard that word since... high school English class." He shook his head with a warm expression in his brown eyes.

"Oh, um, I'm a reader," I said and looked down at my cleaning. Guys that looked like him typically didn't like-

"That's awesome. What do you read? I'm more of a horror fan, myself," he said while fanning himself with the wilted lettuce he had pulled from the shelf.

"I love a good romance novel," I said with a blush.

"Spicy or not spicy?" he asked, his expression mischievous.

I smiled. "Spicy, of course."

"It's always the quiet ones," he chuckled.

The sprinklers above the lettuce kicked on with a *hiss* and he bent back to get his curls wet.

"What are you doing?!"

"It's waking me up," he said and gargled some of the water before swallowing it. He stretched his neck back to reach the water and his throat bobbed almost obscenely as he swallowed.

"I thought you were turning this into a wet t-shirt party," I giggled, tearing my eyes away from his throat and accidentally locking on his damp chest.

"We could," Benjamin said with waggling brows.

I laughed and returned to restocking the now clean apple bin. "Maybe we could get Oscar to let us wear our pajamas."

"Nah, we wouldn't want that," he said as the sprinklers turned off.

"Because we'd fall asleep?"

Benjamin approached me and shook his wet curly head, spraying me with droplets of cold water, and took an apple from my hand. "Because I sleep naked." He took a bite of the apple, sucked up the juice, winked, and walked away.

I finished my shift unsteady on my feet.

Monday was the first day off from work that I didn't spend at school in a long time. After getting home from work just after five, I could sleep in. I didn't want to sleep the day away, so I made sure I was up at noon. I spent the day off in my pajamas and reading a great romantic suspense novel on my Kindle.

The romantic interest in the book I was reading was described as tall, dark, and handsome, but I kept picturing Benjamin. I couldn't help it- my crush was intense.

Tuesday was another night shift. It was silly, but I was looking forward to going to work. I picked out a low-cut V-neck t-shirt and put on more eye make-up than I typically wore on a workday. Before I left home, I spritzed on some perfume. I hoped I didn't see Donna today; she would never let me live it down.

I had lost the bet last shift and had to pick up coffee for Benjamin today. So, I was gripping a huge mocha drink when I got to work. Benjamin's eyes widened as he saw me come in the door. He put his keys in his locker before slamming it shut and leaning back against it.

"Oh, Layla, you beautiful thing, you," he said as I approached him with his drink.

He's talking about coffee. He's talking about coffee. He's talking about *coffee*.

I giggled but stopped short when his fingers brushed against mine as he took his drink. My throat tightened, and I involuntarily clenched my legs together. A man had not affected me this much since I was a hormone crazed teenager.

"Did you sleep in yesterday?" he asked casually as I got my apron from my locker.

"Just until noon, I didn't want to be too far off my usual schedule," I said as we took turns clocking in. "You?"

He shrugged. "I got nervous about it and ended up not going to sleep until after my gym time. So like six yesterday evening."

"Wait, you were awake for over twenty-four hours?" I said incredulously.

"Yeah, and then slept until almost noon today," he laughed. "I'll have to follow your schedule and sleep with you."

I knew what he meant. He meant he would sleep when I slept.

But I could not convince my body of this, and I tripped over my feet and exclaimed, "You sleep naked!"

"That I do," he said, side eyeing me with a smirk as we approached the front of the store.

"It's- it's a lot of time naked," I tried to say casually but stuttered and gestured awkwardly in the air.

"Some might say it's not *enough* time," Benjamin said lowly as he opened the front office door.

I rolled my eyes to look as though his words did not affect me.

"What's not enough time?" Oscar asked from his position at the manager's desk. Our day shift manager, Hal, went home at five and usually Benjamin was there to work until close. Since Benjamin was the overnight manager today, Oscar filled in until our nine o'clock shift.

"To read all the books on our lists, Oscar," Benjamin said happily.

Oscar shrugged off our conversation and leaned back in his chair. "Tonight, I want the meat case to be deep cleaned. I had Donna leave out the cleaner she used the last time in the supply closet. And Benjamin, keep Layla in line of sight."

"How come he doesn't have to clean?" I asked, and crossed my arms. "Oscar, are you being misogynistic?"

Oscar's mustache practically walked off of his face in his outraged shock. Benjamin elbowed me in the ribs, and I fought back my laugh. "No!" Oscar gasped. "I only meant he should choose a task where he can see you. To keep you safe!"

"She's kidding," Benjamin said and elbowed me again.

Oscar's face turned red in irritation as I laughed.

The night had cooled enough that Benjamin opened up the

front doors after we finished our cleaning tasks. We sat on the stools from the registers at the open doors for a water break.

"I thought staying active all night would help me stay awake, but the sleep itch is so strong," I said with a yawn as the wind blew in softly. It cooled the sweat on my brow and chest, and I shivered.

"Did you change your soap or shampoo?" Benjamin asked suddenly.

"No, why?" I said and self consciously touched my hair.

He gave a sniff. "You smell different. Was it your laundry soap?"

I shook my head. "Oh, I'm wearing perfume."

"Hm," he said with a quick, involuntary scrunch of his nose.

"I won't wear it anymore," I said with finality.

"It's not bad, but..." he said but trailed off with a shrug. "I like your usual smell."

Mildly embarrassed over my smell, I got up from my seat to go back to work.

"Don't go far," Benjamin called back to me.

"I don't think Oscar meant for you to follow me to the bathroom," I said sarcastically.

"He might have. I'd rather be safe than sorry," he said, mimicking my tone and getting up from his stool.

I giggled and went to the bathroom alone, before returning to my task.

4

Benjamin and I developed a steady rhythm of working our overnight shifts. We were professional, though friendly, towards each other and worked efficiently together. It had been a few months of uneventful evenings stretched into the early hours of the morning. We each had a task to do in the evening and we would typically finish and sit together and read for the rest of the shift. My crush on him grew, of course, but I kept myself together. It seemed clear that he was not interested in me, so I remained quietly and respectfully entranced. One time in August, he wore a tank top, and I had to spend time with my head in the ice cream freezer.

We spent our months of nights competing to build elaborate displays of sale items, racing to wax the floor, having eating competitions with day-old pastry items, and talking about the books we were reading. The flow of customers was slow. Most nights, there were only a few people coming in to do some late-night shopping. Most of them being third shift workers, frantic parents, and a few insomniacs. Oscar let us continue our overnight shifts with our raises the entire summer, and as the season cooled, we knew it was likely to end. I had saved more money to put towards my store. Even if Oscar stopped the overnight shifts, I knew that Benjamin and I had formed a friendship that would last after our quiet nights.

Saturday was the rib cookout and end of summer party and it truly was feeling like fall. Today, as we walked into work, it had been dark for a few hours, and there were no more summer fireflies in the air. Benjamin greeted me with a pumpkin spice latte, since I had won last shift's display competition. I had shaped a pencil out of canned goods and corn and Oscar was so tickled I got at least two delighted mustache twitches.

The local college was starting up again, and the students kept all hours. It was near midnight when I had a line of frat boys at my register. Benjamin stayed in the front manager's office, doing his own work, but was within earshot of my conversations. The boys were rambunctious, most were friendly enough, buying snack foods and beer for their back-to-school parties. When most of them had left and waited in the parking lot, a few remained. They were snickering quietly to themselves as they approached my register. I knew this to be a sign of trouble and took a breath.

"Did you find everything okay?" I asked as I started ringing out their bags of potato chips.

"Everything except a date for a party," one guy said, and leaned his elbows on the small payment platform. His brown hair was gelled within an inch of its life and his green eyes held a confidence that he was about to succeed in his mission.

"Did you check produce?" I asked lightly.

"Huh?" he asked and tilted his head like a puppy. Most

women probably considered him good looking, but I really only had eyes for Benjamin these days.

"Never mind," I said with a smirk.

"Well, what do you think, wanna ditch work and come to a party?" he asked and leaned even further into my space.

"No, thanks," I said and continued to ring their purchases.

His friends guffawed and slapped each other's chests.

"Your total is twenty-three-"

"No, I think you're going to give me the friends and family discount, since we're dating," he said with a grin and a wink.

"We are not. Your total-"

"Is nothing."

"That's stealing."

His friends were beside themselves with laughter.

"My form of payment is sexual," he said, and winked back at his friends.

"I only accept payment in cash or card," I said with a sigh and a bored look.

"Has anyone ever told you that you're frigid?" he asked, his face hardening. "I bet I can warm you up."

"I'm fine," I replied, and opened my hand for payment. "Twenty-three-"

"Or I could beat it out of you-" the frat guy snarled, and his friends *oohed* excitedly behind him.

"Twenty-three, ninety-seven," I said quietly and as steadily as I could. I could only fake my confidence knowing Benjamin was listening and could provide backup.

"Like I said, I only pay in sexual favors," the guy said and walked around the counter.

I could hear the squeak of Benjamin getting out of his seat. "And like I said, *I* don't accept sexual favors. He, on the other hand, might." I pointed back to where Benjamin came out of the manager's office.

The guy and his friends looked to where tall, tattooed, muscular, and incredibly pissed off Benjamin was approaching. His face was stony, with a clenched jaw and furrowed brow. Even I felt intimidated, and he was on my side. I smirked at the frat guys as they dropped their purchases on the belt.

"So? What's the favor?" Benjamin asked in a low, menacing tone.

The frat guy stepped back and tried for the "aw come on, man" shrug. "It's nothing, dude."

"Get the fuck out. Do not come back," Benjamin said and gripped the edge of the bagging area so hard his knuckles turned white.

The guys ran out without making purchases and met with their more respectful friends in the parking lot. When the door shut with a *whoosh* of crisp autumn air and the bell tinkled, I finally let out a breath. Benjamin walked to the door and made sure they all drove off. When the last car left the parking lot, I plopped down onto my stool. Benjamin whirled around to face me.

"Are you okay, Layla?" he asked, his voice back to normal.

"Yeah," I croaked as I realized my mouth had gone dry. My heart was still beating out a fast rhythm, and I was sure I was red and sweating.

While I was sure that was a common occurrence for many women, or even a mild version of what some experience, that was a big deal for this little town. I had experienced nothing quite like it, and I knew I was lucky. But the feelings of fear and violation didn't go away just knowing that fact. Benjamin came over to me and put a hand on my shoulder. "You sure?"

I nodded. "I guess it's been a while since I've been hit on," I said, trying to minimize the situation to avoid awkwardness with Benjamin.

"Um, are you kidding? That was seconds away from assault," he scolded like I was insane.

I nodded. "I know, sorry. I just... that was weird. And scary. Thank you for saving me."

"I am pretty heroic, aren't I?" he asked, and puffed up his chest. "They ran like scared puppies."

"We might need a mop to clean up their piss," I giggled and tried not to ogle his chest. I was shaken up, not immune.

"Get the mop!" he shouted and then picked up the store's microphone and said, "Clean up on aisle frat boy. It's a big puddle, we need something heavy duty. Bring Oscar's mustache!"

I was laughing and feeling slightly better now. I kicked at him playfully as he put the microphone back.

"On a more serious note, I do not, actually, accept sexual favors as payment," he said and was backing away towards the office.

"I know. Only Donna's peanut butter bars," I replied seriously.

He threw his head back with a shouted "FUCK! I'm hungry for those bars! I would do sexual favors *for* those bars!"

"I'll let Donna know," I said casually as I gathered the dropped bags of chips and cases of beer.

"Oh, she knows," he said dismissively and went into the office.

I laughed for a long time at that as I put away the discarded snacks.

Later, while I was bleary-eyed and staring out the window I had just cleaned, Benjamin approached me with a yawn.

"You said earlier it had been a while since you'd been hit on," he stated and leaned against the window so his temple rested against the glass I had just cleaned.

"Indeed," I answered, not sure where this was going.

"Indubitably," he shot back on reflex. "But... how long?"

He lifted his head, and a smudge was present on my clean glass. I sprayed it and wiped it down. "I don't know, maybe a year. Why?"

"Just wondering," he said with another yawn and rested his head against the glass again.

"What about you?" I asked, eyeing where his head rested against my newly re-cleaned glass.

"I was hit on getting your coffee today," he replied.

"That's nice." I tried not to sound bratty.

He quirked an eyebrow and lifted his head from the glass again. I sprayed it and wiped it down and looked pointedly at him.

"Are you trying to make me jealous?" I asked, trying to figure out his angle.

"Jealous?" he asked with a further quirk of his eyebrow.

"Yeah, that you get hit on more than I do." I blushed, realizing he might have thought I said that I was jealous other people hit on him because I wanted him. It was true, but that wasn't my intended meaning.

"Oh, no," he said and rested his head, yet again, on my glass. "I was just making conversation."

"Okay," I sighed. "Can you not do that?" I pointed to where his head was smudging up my glass. "I've cleaned it multiple times now."

"I know. You wrinkled your nose every time I messed it up. It was cute," he said with a grin as he walked away.

I whipped him on the butt with the rag I was holding.

He let out a fake, high-pitched moan and kept walking. "Oh, Oscar! Your mustache chafes!"

Our next shift was another overnight, and I brought him a coffee and a big peanut butter cookie from Beans & Leaves. I also had a book in hand that I thought he might like. My heart leapt when I saw him already clocking in when I entered the staff door.

"Hey," he said before looking up. His eyes lit up when he saw I was armed with goodies.

"Hey. I, um, wanted to thank you. You know, for offering to accept sexual favors as payment on my behalf. It was very honorable." I felt my face heat and handed him his gifts.

He blushed, too. His cheeks going all blotchy.

"It's your favorite mocha. And- and a peanut butter cookie. It's not Donna's bake, but it's the best I could do without adopting a corgi from her. I asked. And, um, this is a book that made me think of you. It's kind of horror," I mumbled, with a few awkward shrugs. I was standing squarely, but felt sure I was about to trip over my own feet.

"Kind of horror?" He questioned.

"It's also a romance."

"Is it spicy?" he asked with a waggle of his brows.

I blushed harder. "Yeah, but there's more to it than that."

"Baby, did you just give me porn?"

Fire. I was on fire. Sweat burst from every pore. I gave an awkward exhale as an attempt at a laugh.

"How spicy are we talking here? On a scale from Oscar's mustache after Flamin' Hot Cheetos to Oscar's mustache after Atomic Wings at Scoot's?"

"Uh," I said and tried to discreetly wipe the sweat from my top lip. "Wings."

"Are you a freak, Layla Avery?" he asked in a shocked whisper.

I gave a dry swallow. All of my body's moisture was currently in my armpits and on my face. I tried to give a coquettish one shoulder shrug with batting eyelashes but likely looked like I was having a fit.

"I knew it," he said with a dark satisfaction and put the book and cookie in his locker. He turned back to me with a soft expression now. "Thank you for the thank you gifts. But please know that I would never let someone mistreat you like that." He tucked a strand of my hair behind my ear. "I would have beaten those assholes to a pulp if they didn't run off."

Oh my god, so maybe he could be the Morally Gray Romance Hero that he looked like. My brain had entirely fizzled out at his light touch so I could only stare, doe eyed, up at him. I was suddenly aware of how the toes of our shoes were almost touching. His hand lingered near my jaw, and he locked his brown eyes on mine. If I was sweating and hot before, I was now hot and sweating for an entirely different reason. He tucked my hair a second time and stroked down my jawline to my chin, where he pinched it lightly before letting go and stepping back. The scent of his deodorant surrounded me still and filled my lungs when I took a long, steadying inhale. I put my keys in my locker and put my apron on with shaking hands before following him into the store to start our shift. It was hours before I cooled off.

5

Thursday was a day shift for me and Benjamin, and it was beautifully bright. It was the kind of sunshiny weather that had Oscar handing ice cream to every child that came into the store. It wasn't hot out, and Oscar was getting rid of some summer overstock, but the children loved it. Donna was pulling out the fall and Halloween decorations while I worked the register. She untangled garlands of warm-colored autumn leaves while we chatted about her recent corgi rescue and caught up with the customers who came in the slower morning hours.

Benjamin and Oscar were working on something for an upcoming event, and I could hear their voices coming from the manager's office. I couldn't help but be acutely aware, *bodily* aware of where Benjamin was in the store. The scent of his deodorant and hair product was ingrained on my consciousness like an absolute stalker. I needed to get it together.

Later, Donna and I took lunch together, like usual, at the picnic table outside the store. We were typically quiet during our lunches, saving our chatting time for when we were on the clock and Oscar had to pay us to gossip. I was engrossed in reading when I felt a little, sharp tug on the end of my ponytail. Benjamin was joining us at the table and my stomach instantly clenched in anticipation.

"I started that book," he murmured as if it were a secret, leaning towards me as he sat down close to me.

"Oh, yeah?" My voice was deceivingly airy. "What do you think so far?"

He gave a side eye to see if Donna was paying attention, and her eyes on her phone fooled him. She was most definitely listening, and he was an idiot not to know that, honestly. She lit a cigarette and winked at me when Benjamin looked away from her and opened his energy drink with a *snap*.

"I am in disbelief that you read that," he said quietly. When he spoke quietly, his voice rumbled, and I swore I could feel its vibrations between my legs.

"I don't always read horror," I said with a shrug. "But sometimes I like the darker themes thrown in with my romance."

He shook his head in awe. "I figured you for the lovey-dovey sugary sweet stuff."

"A girl can have a broad range of interests, Benjamin," I said with mock insult.

"How broad are we talking?" he asked suggestively and looked over my body while waggling his eyebrows. He took a long swig of his carbonated energy drink, still waggling his eyebrows over the can.

I laughed. "If that was supposed to be an innuendo about my body, try again."

He laughed, too. "Layla, there are whips and chains in this book. Knife play! I ask you for the second time since you gave me this book. Nay, I *plead* with you for an answer: how freaky are you?"

Donna coughed in her cloud of cigarette smoke. It wasn't unusual behavior for her, but I had known her long enough to read her coughs like I could read Oscar's mustache. She was shocked and amused. I knew I was blushing, and I looked down at the rather cozy fantasy romance I had been reading. Covering the book with my hands, I looked up at Benjamin through my lashes. "I'd rather not say," I whispered, not sure why I was even answering his question. I was a total idiot.

Benjamin was staring, wide-eyed at me like I'd actually just shocked him with my mostly joking answer.

Donna cackled and stubbed out her finished cigarette. "You two would make a cute couple, you know."

"Who, us?" Benjamin asked her like he'd never considered it.

Donna nodded and gestured between Benjamin and me.

I was frozen in my seat and could only shake my head with what I hoped to be an aloof expression on my face.

Benjamin chuckled. "Donna, Donna, Donna! Don't you know that I'm just waiting for you! Drop that husband of yours and come to me!"

Oscar leaned out the door with an irritated twitch of his mustache. "Benjamin! Your break is after theirs! I haven't finished showing you that spreadsheet!"

"But I wanted to be with my girl!" Benjamin said dramatically as he stood up to leave. He squeezed my shoulder as he walked behind me and back towards the store.

"You see her at night. Now, come on, I wanted to show

you how I balance the work orders," Oscar said with a wave of his hand.

"Who? Layla? No, Donna is my girl," Benjamin replied and turned back to blow Donna a kiss before going into the store with Oscar.

A blush stained Donna's leathery skin as we both sat in silence for a moment. I quietly reopened my book.

"Peaches, that boy likes you, you know," she stated and lit another cigarette.

I shook my head and traced my finger over my bookmark. "Not like you are suggesting."

"He flirts with you," Donna said and took a long drag.

"He flirts with everyone. He was just flirting with you," I said dismissively.

"He's a flirt, yes. But he looks at you like he looks at my peanut butter bars," Donna said with a laugh as she stood up, crushing her empty tea can to throw away.

I remembered Benjamin saying that he once hid away in Oscar's office and ate ashy peanut butter bars like an animal. And I had a sudden and incredibly vivid mental image of him hiding away in the office to devour *me* like a starved animal. Shaking my head, I cleared up my lunch. "It's not like that," I told Donna as we went back to work.

"If you say so," she said with a scoff.

The rest of my shift was uneventful and rather typical. We all talked about our participation in the upcoming Apple Festival and parade. We were to have a float in the parade and a stand at the festival. Oscar loved planning elaborate events and costumes, so we were not to find out the theme until we got closer to the date. It wasn't unusual to show up to an Oscar planned event to be handed a costume and told your role on the spot. He was the only person, other than myself, to know my clothes sizes. I trusted him to make choices on my behalf for costumes. Donna had once traumatized him by telling him, "Just let me know if I need to get a wax before I show up" when he made our costumes a surprise the first time. Thankfully, our costumes have always been modest and appropriate.

Oscar was thoroughly delighted, hearing us come up with elaborate ideas for what we thought he was planning for the float. Everything from a huge, real apple pie on wheels to the evil apple from Snow White- complete with a fog machine and Donna's witchy cackling. He even added to our scheming because he loved the dramatics of it.

Greg, from the pharmacy next door, came through to pick up some dinner near the end of my shift. "Hello, Layla. I haven't seen you much lately," he said kindly.

"Oh, I've been working nights still," I replied as I rang out his items.

"I hope you've been taking your vitamins. Many people who work third shift don't get enough vitamin D," Greg said and handed me his money.

"Did someone say Vitamin D?" Benjamin asked as he rolled backwards in his chair from the front office.

"You, too, Benjamin," Greg said. "I was just telling Layla that many people who work at night don't get adequate Vitamin D. I can bring over a good multivitamin for the both of you."

"Greg, my man, do you see this?" Benjamin asked and stood

to flex his arms. "Does this look like I eat crap food and not get adequate vitamins?"

I giggled and handed Greg his change. I knew for a fact that Benjamin actually ate unhealthy food regularly.

"Before your night shift, what are you eating?" Greg asked, ignoring Benjamin's flexing.

"It's funny you mention that," I said. "I'm never sure if I should eat breakfast or dinner. I alternate based on my mood."

"I want you to be eating salmon, or drinking a fortified orange juice," Greg said and gathered his bags.

"Sounds like brunch to me," Benjamin said and leaned on my bagging area. "I know a place that does all day brunch not far from here. Want to go before our shift on Sunday?"

"M-me?" I asked and almost dropped the carton of eggs I was ringing out for the next customer.

"Yes," Benjamin said, his brown eyes crinkling in a smile.

"Oh, uh, yeah, sure," I said, my voice squeaking slightly on the "sure."

"Cool," he said and knocked his fist on the edge of the bagging area. "It's a date."

And with that, he walked away. Greg was leaving the store and winked at Donna who nodded back at him. Meddlers- the both of them.

The young mom in my line was gawking at me as I clumsily rang and bagged her items. "No way!" she squealed quietly when Benjamin was back in the office.

"Did he just-?" I asked her.

"Yes, girl. Yes, he did!" she exclaimed.

Was I dreaming? I'd have to look up later if a Vitamin D

deficiency caused hallucinations. My shift ended in a blur and I clocked out without speaking to anyone. I had a date to obsess and shop for.

6

A few hours before our Sunday overnight shift, I met Benjamin in the parking lot of Oscar's. We met there, knowing we'd be coming back to work after our date. I wore a yellow sundress that I had bought ages ago. It had little flowers on it and hung in loose but flattering waves around my thighs. I had healthy curves and was what most would consider "midsize," so the dress hung higher on my legs than it had on the thin model who wore it online. I hadn't worn it yet because of its length- or lack thereof. Worn with white Keds and my brown hair in loose curls, it was definitely a date dress. This was a *date* date right? I needed to clarify in some way with Benjamin. Otherwise, I was going to look stupid.

I tugged self-consciously at the hem of my dress that now felt like something one of the girls from Edible Entertainment would wear. No shame towards them, it just typically wasn't my style, and I was really feeling it as I approached Benjamin. He was still in his car, looking at his phone as I approached him. Bass from his music made the windows vibrate even though the volume was low. He didn't see me approach, so I took a moment to check my hair and makeup in my reflection in his window. I had worn a flirty, dewy makeup look with some autumn colors to match my dress.

I knocked lightly on his window, but he didn't hear me. I didn't want to knock any harder and break his window, so I opened his car door instead. He startled and then looked me over. His eyes trailed a slow, burning path down my body and back up to my face. I tried not to blush and toed my sneaker on the ground and bit my lip.

"Hey," Benjamin said and got out of the car, leaving it running. "You look…"

"Like a waitress from Edible Entertainment, I'm increasingly aware," I tried to laugh it off.

"I was going to say 'gorgeous' but if you were going for 'edible' I could get on board," he said lowly and touched the ends of my hair where it swirled around my shoulders.

"Um, thanks," I said hoarsely. "You look good, too."

And he did. He was wearing a pair of dark wash jeans that clung to his thighs, a black t-shirt, and a black and white flannel. His tattoos on his neck peeked out, and I was struck with the mental image of me tracing the lines with my tongue. I shook the image out and bit my lip again. His brown eyes were fixated on my mouth as he thanked me.

Someone whistled behind us, and I turned to see Donna coming out the back door of the store. She was getting off her shift and leaving for the day. "Hey, Donna," Benjamin and I echoed.

"You two are here early," Donna said like she didn't know damn well that we were going on a date before our shift.

"I'm taking Layla here out before our shift," Benjamin replied.

"Oh, like a date?" Donna asked, and honestly, I was so thankful she was here to meddle.

"I think so," Benjamin said in a way that suggested he wanted it to be a date and he was just waiting on my confirmation.

That meant he was interested in me. Not likely as obsessive as I was, I was sure. I had actual Benjamin radar and could tell anyone where he was when we worked together based on my bodily awareness of him. I tried to play it cool and smiled up at him hesitantly. He smirked down at me as though I'd just given him all the confirmation he needed.

"I knew it! I knew it," Donna laughed as she unlocked her car. "You two have fun. And remember, we have cameras in the store now."

She got into her car cackling and coughing.

Blushing crimson, I took a deep breath. "Well, are you ready to go?" I asked him.

"Very ready," he said and walked around to the passenger side and opened the door for me. "M'lady."

"Please don't say that." I giggled and slid into his car.

"Let me just tip my fedora," he continued and mimed doing just that. His blonde hair was clean and styled in a nicer, more coiffed version of his normal curly haired look. He did that for our *date*.

He gently closed my door and ran around to the driver's side and got in. His car smelled like him. Old Spice deodorant, clean soap, his pine scented hair product, and a little of male sweat. But not a stinky sweat. The kind that smelled like pure pheromones and made me almost crazy.

"Alright, so this place is a bit of a drive. Maybe thirty minutes, but it's right by the lake and has the salmon and orange juice Greg said you needed," Benjamin said as he turned his music down further and pulled out of the parking lot.

"*We* needed," I corrected.

"I am in perfect health," Benjamin said with mock defensiveness.

"But I look malnourished and sickly?" I gestured to myself.

"No, you do not," he said and looked me over again, his eyes lingering on where my dress rode up my thighs while sitting in the car. I was suddenly heavily aware of the sploot my thighs did when I was sitting. I tugged on my dress and shifted in my seat. "You look fantastic," he elaborated and returned his eyes to the road.

We chatted about work and some local gossip while Benjamin drove. I was a little fidgety thinking about how I was on a date with Benjamin, so we kept much of our conversation light and safe.

The restaurant Benjamin was taking me to was right on the lake, with a patio over the water. Once we had parked, Benjamin ran around the car to open my door. He took my hand to help me out and as my fingers slid into his palm and he closed his hand around me, a slow heat spread over my body. It was an internal heat that settled in my hips and left my exposed skin in goosebumps. I realized then that I was dumb to not bring a cardigan. Maybe I would just cuddle into Benjamin.

We weaved through a group of people near the hostess stand that was outside on the sidewalk. The flowers in the beds around the restaurant were still in bloom despite the cooler temperature and the surroundings were spotless and manicured. A group of girls were taking posed selfies under a rose arbor next to the door. Some of them stopped to look at Benjamin. I couldn't blame them; he truly was a beautiful man. I felt his hand brush the small of my back, just above the swell of my ass. He leaned down to my ear, his breath hot against my neck. "Do you want to get a picture?"

"It looks occupied," I said breathlessly at the smallest of touches.

He hummed and steered me towards the arbor and group of young women. Many of those women were still gawking at him. "Excuse me, ladies. Would you mind if we snuck in for a quick picture?" He turned on his grocery store charm for them.

They tittered their acceptances and moved out of the way for us. We stood in the arbor and snapped a few selfies. Mostly me smiling big and Benjamin smirking. But then he yanked me close by my waist so that the front of our bodies were flush together, dipped me back, and kissed my cheek near my jaw. I was sure I was gasping in the picture he snapped. I was unaware of our surroundings as he let me stand back up and our bodies were still pressed together. He smirked down at me, and I saw that ferocious blush blotching over his cheeks and neck. I wondered if his whole body blushed. My face burned where his lips had touched, and I resisted the urge to reach up and touch it.

"I'm sending that one to Donna," he said quietly, studying my face. His hands came up to where mine were curled in his shirt. I hadn't even realized that I was gripping him. I swallowed down my embarrassment as he uncurled my fingers, and I stepped back.

"She'll get it printed," I gave a breathy laugh.

We went to walk to the hostess stand, and I noticed the young women who had been taking selfies were still around us and staring. Some with open contempt towards me, some staring lustfully at Benjamin, and some looking shocked. Was it really that upsetting to see a tattooed hunk of a man with a curvy bookworm?

The hostess seated us inside but near the long windows overlooking the lake. It was maybe an hour until sunset, but we were sure to get a good view of it. Benjamin and I sat facing each other. The sun was warm on us despite the chill of the over air-conditioned restaurant. I looked around at the new and trendy place. It looked as though they were aiming for the crisp white farmhouse décor that many people preferred lately. It was brightly lit and smelled clean and like breakfast food. The menu was all brunch style foods and my stomach rumbled as we looked over the thick cardstock.

"Have you been here before?" I asked Benjamin after we ordered coffee and mimosas.

"No, but I had heard about it. It's not really my scene," he said with a hint of his own self-consciousness.

"Not enough tattoos and motorcycles?" I asked.

"Something like that." He shrugged.

"Speaking of tattoos," I started. "When did you get your first one?"

He grinned and sat back in his chair. "When I was sixteen. I did it myself."

"Can I see it?" I asked, leaning forward in my seat.

He unbuttoned the cuff of his flannel on his left sleeve and rolled the material up. I had seen his forearms many times, but the slow reveal of muscle and inked skin was a tantalizing experience. He pointed to a crudely and unevenly drawn skull and crossbones on the top of his forearm and rested his arm on the table. It was enveloped by his other tattoos in his sleeve but not covered up. "I thought I was such a badass," he said fondly.

"I bet you were," I said and reached out and lightly traced my finger over his oldest tattoo. Goosebumps rose on his skin, and I felt emboldened to trail my fingers along his skin, down his arm as I pulled my hand back into my lap. The light gold hairs on his arm caught the light and made his tattoos seem like they were sparkling.

"I wasn't," he chuckled. "But thank you."

Our mimosas and coffee were delivered, and both were delicious. We ordered the Best of Brunch meal that was served family style. The waitress warned us politely that it was typically for tables of six to eight people.

"We'll be up all night and will need the leftovers," Benjamin said lightly to the waitress as he handed her our menus.

She looked shocked between Benjamin and me and back with a blush. He wasn't wrong, but this girl did not know that we worked third shift at a small-town grocery store. She probably thought he meant we would be up all-night having sex with leftover pancake and bacon breaks. Suddenly, I wanted nothing more than to slap a closed sign on the door to Oscar's and drag Benjamin home to my apartment.

"Oh, um, okay," she said meekly and took the menus and left quickly.

"She thinks were going home to have sex and eat pancakes,"

I hissed to him over the table when she left. I couldn't help but laugh.

He chuckled like he knew exactly what she thought he meant. "That sounds like a great night. Sex and leftovers."

I didn't know what to say, so I sat back in my seat and sipped my mimosa. He was still smirking at me.

"So, tell me why you agreed to work overnights at Oscar's," he said in a quiet voice and leaned forward with his arms on the table towards me.

When I set down my mimosa glass, he reached out his fingers and caressed the back of my hand. I shivered and had to repeat his question in my head.

"I want to open a bookstore with a café. I needed to save up more money," I replied after a moment.

"That's... perfect for you," he said, his eyes warm. "Are you close to your goal?"

I shrugged. "I'm not sure, really. It depends on the real estate. And I have to do some more research on distributors."

"I can help a little with the distributors stuff. When I do the ordering for Oscar's I can see the local networks for distributors. Tonight, I'll have you come look," he offered and sipped his coffee. The mug was a little vintage teacup and looked kind of ridiculous in his large, tattooed hand.

"That would be great, thanks," I said gratefully. "So, why are you doing overnights?"

"My goals are actually pretty similar to yours. I want to open a tattoo shop," he said.

"Wait, you tattoo? Like you're the artist?" I asked, shocked and looking down at the poorly done skull and crossbones.

He laughed. "That was a long time ago. Here," he pulled his phone from his pocket and opened up an album of tattoos. "I've done these."

He handed me the phone, warm from his body heat, and I looked through the pictures. He was really talented. There were some incredible pieces of mostly black ink and impressively realistic pictures on many people. A lot of them women. I felt suddenly self-conscious, realizing I looked nothing like the women in these pictures. "You tattoo a lot of people," I mumbled as I scrolled.

"I don't tattoo women I'm dating, if that's what you're thinking," he said in a low voice, scrutinizing my face.

I shook my head as if he hadn't just pinned me with the truth. "Would you tattoo me?" The words came out of my mouth without censoring. I had never really thought of getting a tattoo before. I had pierced ears that closed up every few years that I got pierced again, so I'd been in tattoo parlors before. But nothing ever seemed important enough to me to make it permanent on my skin.

"Absolutely not," he said darkly.

"Wh-why?" I asked, turning wide eyes up to him.

"Nobody ever gets just one tattoo. They're like Pringles," he said, his voice less dark but still tinged with something unfamiliar. "If I gave you one, you would want more. And you might get them from someone else and I couldn't bear to see someone else's mark on your skin."

I tried to keep my voice light. "Don't people have their own tattoo artists? Like they have their favorite hair stylists? They always get their tattoos from the same person and hair by the same person."

"Some people do, sure," he said, his eyes bouncing to points all over my face.

"Well, maybe you could be... mine," I suggested, the last word coming out as a whisper.

Benjamin let out a breath that ghosted over my face and leaned back in his seat. He rubbed his hands over his face and then adjusted his jeans. "No," he said, his voice gravelly.

I was about to ask why, when our waitress appeared with a smile and an enormous platter of food. She set everything down, crowding our small table. She left quickly after serving us. I looked to Benjamin over the plates of food, my eyes wide.

He grinned. "I don't know where to begin."

The food looked fantastic and smelled even better. We ate quietly for a few moments before I took a bite of some pancakes that were made with peanut butter. I moaned through my bite and Benjamin's eyes snapped up to me. "It's peanut butter!" I explained. Benjamin opened his mouth expectantly, and I laughed and cut him a bite and fed it to him.

"So, if I showed up to your tattoo shop, without an idea of what I wanted, what would you suggest?" I asked him.

"I would suggest you go home and think about it," he said easily. "Not every tattoo has to have some sort of deep meaning, but you shouldn't leave it up to someone who doesn't know you."

"No, I meant *me* me. Not someone you didn't know," I clarified.

"Oh, I'd still tell you to go home," Benjamin replied.

"Why?" I asked.

"You don't have any tattoos, so I would want your first one to be meaningful," he said with a shrug.

"Well, I want you to be my first," I said lightly and sipped my mimosa.

Benjamin swallowed his food hard and took a long gulp of coffee before I realized the innuendo. I smirked at him then, feeling seductive.

"Do you want to go for a walk on the beach after we're done? We still have time," Benjamin said, changing the topic.

"Yes, I'd love that. It's been too long since I've been at the lake," I said happily.

We boxed up our numerous leftovers, got coffees to go, and headed out to Benjamin's car. He had picked up the tab and denied me pitching in for the bill. We put our bag of leftovers in the car and Benjamin pulled his leather jacket out of the backseat for me. He slung it over my shoulders and fixed my hair, so it wasn't trapped under the collar. I inhaled the scent of leather and *him*.

We carried our coffees and shoes down to the lake and walked along the beach at the water's edge. There were other couples and families watching the sunset, but I still felt alone with Benjamin. We had technically been alone together many times before, but this was different. We stood at the edge of the water and watched in silence as the sun dipped behind the water on the horizon. Couples around us kissed and took pictures, children squealed in excitement to see the sunset, and I looked up at Benjamin. His brown eyes warm with a golden glow as the last rays of sunlight reached us on the shore. He smiled down at me and I licked my lips, anticipating a kiss. My heart thumped hard in my chest as

I waited. He didn't lean down to kiss me, despite my upturned face. "We should head back. It's going to get cold quickly."

Wordlessly, I nodded and walked with him, shoulder to shoulder up the beach and to his car. I felt a pit in my stomach, and an awareness of my foolishness for thinking Benjamin was going to kiss me. I had seen pictures of the women he associated with, and they were much more beautiful and daring than a bookworm grocery store clerk. As we got back to his car, I remained silent, stewing in my dejection. He opened the door for me and leaned down, one hand bracing himself on the open door and his eyes level with mine. "Have you ever gone to work directly after a date?" he asked.

"Not a first date, no," I huffed out a laugh. "An established relationship might have started the day with a breakfast date or a lunch date before work or school. But not a first date."

"Is that what this is? A first date?" he asked quietly and studied my face.

I swallowed. "Technically, yeah. I've never been on a date with you before," I said awkwardly. Then I realized that he might have been trying to see if I was as uninterested as he was. "Or, I mean, friend date. Co-worker date. Or whatever."

He smiled and slid his jacket off of my shoulders and tossed it in the back seat.

"It was a date," he clarified, his expression mostly unreadable despite his smile.

"A *date* date?" I asked with a sigh.

"I thought that was established," he said looking confused.

"Oh, okay, cool," I said and got into the car.

He chuckled and closed the door behind me.

When he got into the car, he handed me his phone. "Pick some music, little co-pilot."

I smiled and found a playlist inspired by the book I had given him. When I set his phone in the cupholder, I placed my hand on my lap. It was in a location that would make it easy for him to hold. If he wanted to, that is. We made the half hour drive in quiet, comfortable conversation. But he did not hold my hand. Despite the way his attention made me and my body feel, he was not interested in me. I needed to accept this. We pulled in at Oscar's and Benjamin smiled at me as we gathered our things to go to work.

"Feel prepared to work all night?" He asked.

I smiled despite my dejected feeling. "Yeah, I'm so sugar and carb loaded. I'll be up all night whether or not I want to."

"Perfect," he grinned and pinched my chin as I looked up at him. And with that, he led the way into the store for our shift.

7

I stopped at my car before we went into Oscar's. I wanted to change out of my dress and into some jeans and a sweater for work. Oscar was up front, and the restroom was occupied, so I stepped into Oscar's office in the back to change. There was only one camera in the back office, and it faced the staff door, so I felt safe changing in the office. Benjamin was already up front, so I needed to hurry before someone came looking for me. I set my clothes down on Oscar's desk and kicked the door shut. It didn't shut all the way, but the staff room was empty, and I was going to be quick. I toed off my Keds and slid my dress up and over my shoulders. I set it down on the desk. When I felt eyes on me, I was just about to grab my cabled knit sweater. I froze and was just about to turn to slam the door shut all the way when I heard keys being softly set in a metal locker. I had heard those specific keys being put into a locker before every single one of my shifts for months. It was Benjamin.

Still frozen, I realized he was watching me as I changed. I should have felt violated. I should have shut the door. I should have gotten dressed quickly. But I didn't. I turned so my back was to the barely open door. I couldn't face the door without making eye contact with Benjamin. So instead, he got a full view of my ass in a high-waisted white thong. I wore a matching white cotton bra with a little pink ribbon between the cups. With my arms above my head, I stretched my body languidly, though my heart was pounding. I stood on tiptoes for a moment in my stretch and to flex the muscles in my thighs and ass. This was so wrong. I was allowing Benjamin to see me unclothed after I had *just* decided to let him go and give him space. Simultaneously, I felt disappointed in myself and completely turned on. Exhibitionism was not something I had thought I'd be engaging in tonight, but here I was.

I ended my stretch by using a hair tie to put my hair up in a ponytail. I normally would have tied my hair up after I was dressed, but that would have been less of a show. Picking up my jeans off the desk, I hesitated a second before I turned to the side to bend and step into them. I heard an audible but very quiet sigh as he must have realized he wasn't getting the full view tonight. Just as well, though. He could have at least held my hand before he saw my entire ass.

Fighting a smirk, I pulled my cream-colored knit sweater over my head and toed back on my Keds. I heard the swinging door to the store open and shut as I exited the office holding my dress. Benjamin was pretending to have just walked into the staff room and he stopped to look me over. His face and neck were blotchy with a fierce blush. I bit my lip to keep in a laugh, but let the corners of my mouth curl up in a smile as I crossed to my locker.

"Oh, you changed," he said casually, like he hadn't just seen me in my panties.

"Yeah, I didn't want to flash any customers," I said and swallowed my laugh. I put my dress in my locker and shut the door.

"Wouldn't want that," he said hollowly.

He was standing in the middle of the staff room, seemingly without purpose.

"Are you okay?" I asked and approached him. I reached a hand out to his arm.

He swallowed, not taking his eyes off of me. "I'm good. Fine."

"You look like you've seen a ghost," I said and looked around us hesitantly. He didn't really look like he'd seen a ghost. He looked like he'd just seen me undressed and was trying to play it cool.

Benjamin shook his head as if he was trying to shake himself out of a stupor. "Just tired, I guess. Shouldn't have had so many carbs before work."

I turned back to my locker for my apron and stretched before putting it on, mirroring my earlier stretch. "I feel great. Though, I'd love to crawl into bed. I just started a great book and I keep thinking about it."

Oscar chose that moment to come through the swinging door. "Hello, Layla."

"Hey, Oscar," I replied. "What's on the schedule tonight?"

"Can you do something with the apple display? I want something wonderful for the Apple Festival. Maybe clean the bins, shine the apples, and make us a nice sign. Don't use the apples in the display. Remember last year when they all fell on Marjorie?"

I shuddered as the image of the old lady under a pile of bruised apples came to mind. "Got it!"

"Benjamin, I left the order list for you on the desk," Oscar directed and gathered his belongings to leave.

"Aye aye, captain," Benjamin said as we went through the swinging doors together. The front door's bell had chimed to let us know someone came in and we would be needed soon.

Benjamin worked up front in the office while I mopped the store. He stopped to ring out the two customers that came in the first half of our shift. We talked little other than to check in that the other was safe and awake for a few hours. I started the apple display after the store was mopped and stocked. I was using chalk paint when Benjamin called over the loudspeaker. "Layla Avery, please come to the manager's office. Layla Avery, to the manager's office."

I was within earshot when he made the call, so the volume startled me enough that I spilled some of the chalk paint on the floor. I turned and gave him a tired and irritated expression, but he only grinned back.

After I cleaned up the spilled paint, I met him in the little front office. "What's up?" I asked him casually.

"You had said you wanted to see some of the ordering and distribution stuff. I just finished our order, but I can show you the process," he said and turned in the creaking office chair.

He slapped his thigh in invitation for me to sit on his lap. Part of my brain was already diving headfirst onto his strong thighs and the other part said to turn and walk away. Outwardly, I walked to his lap and carefully perched sideways on his left thigh. He reached his hands around me to use the keyboard, but the angle was awkward, and he couldn't reach with his left hand around. He gripped my hips, lifted me up a few inches, and spun me so my right leg draped on the other side of his thigh. I was straddling his leg now. He reached around me again to use the keyboard and could reach. He leaned in so he lightly pressed his chest against my back. I kept my breathing steady so he wouldn't notice that I was so worked up by sitting on his lap.

"Okay, so we use a local network of distributors, but it's also connected to a few national ones, too. See, they're along this tab. I just ordered dairy and I know how much we sell in a typical week, so I order that much from our dairy provider. National brands are different..." he was still talking but my brain tuned him out.

I was hyper aware of how his forearm muscles bunched and moved as he worked. He typed on the keyboard and used the mouse and I saw nothing of what he was doing on the computer. I watched his tattooed hands and long fingers move across the keys. I swallowed. My mouth watered, and I had the strongest urge to take his long fingers into my mouth and suck.

His scent surrounded me, and his voice rumbled next to my right ear. I registered none of what he was saying but could nod whenever his tone suggested he was asking a question. I wanted to concentrate on what he was trying to teach me but the proximity of his body and the encompassing scent of him had me unfocused and lust filled. I felt my core clenching around nothing and had the insane urge to rock on his muscled thigh. My controlled breathing was the only thing that moved me. It felt like I had the stereotypical butterflies in my stomach... only lower.

Benjamin rested a hand on my hip and cleared his throat.

"Huh?" I asked. "What was that last bit?" As if I had heard a single word.

"I asked if you, uh, knew any names of some book distributors," he said, his voice sounding strained.

"I have to do a bit more research. I think I go through the publishers?" I said, completely forgetting all the research and companies I had already worked on.

"Hm, well maybe next shift we can look at them," he said, his voice still strained.

"Yeah," I said lamely.

The front door chimed to signal a customer coming in. A screen displaying the security camera feeds was over the desk and showed a woman coming in and grabbing a basket. The crotch of my jeans felt cool as the air hit it when I stood up off his lap. I had been so hot and turned on sitting on his lap that the inside of my jeans was damp. I shook off the feeling of embarrassment- there was no way he had felt that- and went to greet the customer.

The exhausted woman picked up a can of powdered baby formula, ground coffee, and a pack of diapers. These were our most sold items in the middle of the night, other than alcohol and snacks. There was always a tired parent in survival mode. I had a habit of "forgetting" to ring up the coffee they bought and always let them have it for free.

Benjamin and I took our break together in the front office. He let me take the desk chair while he perched on a stool from a register. We ate some of our reheated leftovers and wished for more mimosas and coffee.

"How much are you going to work out to make up for this food?" I asked, trying to make conversation.

"Are you calling me fat?" he quirked an eyebrow at me over a bite of pancake.

"No, I just mean you're always talking about working out. I figured since you look like that, you count your calories," I explained.

"Not really, honestly. Don't tell my gym friends, though. They'd have a fit," he said and finished the pancakes. "I work out to *feel* strong, not for the visible muscles. Seeing them in the mirror is a bonus. I'm strong and healthy, and sometimes I eat like shit. But I will not make myself feel like shit because of it."

"I thought the phrase was 'you are what you eat,'" I snorted and sipped my water.

"Nah. I don't have whiskers or a tail," he said with a naughty wink and smirk.

It took me way too long to understand what he said. I had taken another bite of food, chewed it, swallowed it, and taken another sip of water before it clicked. He had been waiting patiently for the joke to land. I looked up at him on the stool and choked on my water, eyes bugging out.

He laughed. "Took you long enough, little one."

"I thought you meant a cow and that you like to eat beef," I laughed, a blush staining my cheeks.

"No *meat* here," he said.

"Wait, I've seen you eat a cheeseburger, and you just ate bacon."

"Layla, I meant- ugh- another euphemism. 'Meat' meaning

dick. Because I'm not into dudes!" He was laughing now and had to set his plate down.

"I don't think I've ever heard a dick referred to as 'meat!'" I exclaimed, also laughing.

"Well, I'd hope the guys you're hooking up with aren't so vulgar," he said and shook his head.

"I don't mind a little dirty talk," I said without thinking.

"Oh?" he asked, his eyebrow raised in interest.

"Not that I really hook up... with guys," I said. They could have used my blush as a traffic stop.

"Girls?" he asked.

"No, I just mean, I don't really... hook up. It's not my style." I shrugged and looked down.

"Oh, so you like dirty talk in the bedroom from a man you're in a relationship with. You're a kinky little one," he said in a smooth, deep voice. He leaned towards me and watched me intently.

I was sweating now. A quick roll of my eyes and a huffed laugh was all I could muster to show how unaffected I was. This was totally inappropriate, and he's not interested in me. He was just playing with me. Just like he did with everyone.

"Sorry, I didn't mean to make you uncomfortable," he said sincerely.

"It's not- I'm not- I just don't really hook up with guys casually. I prefer to be in a relationship. It's not that I'm super innocent or anything." I tried to sound as unaffected and casual as I could.

"That's respectful. I wasn't making fun of you for it. I just like your blush," he admitted.

I smiled. "Says the guy with the biggest blush I know. Those tattoos on your neck don't really hide it."

"Well, I tried," he chuckled and started cleaning up our finished plates. "Also, cows don't have whiskers."

"They do," I said confidently.

"I'm going to Google it, and loser buys coffee," he said and pulled out his phone.

I waited patiently for my victory as he typed.

"Fucking hell," he laughed.

"I'll take a chai latte," I said breezily and left the office.

I spent the rest of the shift finishing the apple display and tidying up. I created a chalk sign with recipes for each type of apple we carried. Apple pie, appletini, apple walnut salad, and apple cinnamon oat cookies. It was cute, educational, and festive. Exactly what Oscar loved.

When the end of our shift came around, I was exhausted. Benjamin and I were silent as we gathered items from our lockers. His eyes were puffy, like he was fighting sleep, and I knew I was no better off.

"I'm going to fall over," he mumbled to me.

"Me, too," I agreed with a yawn.

"Those carbs didn't work," he said and shut his locker.

"I'll complain to Greg," I said sleepily.

"He told us to eat fish and orange juice," Benjamin corrected.

"Oh. Well, we fucked up then," I said and shut my locker.

Benjamin snorted. "Shoulda brought him with us."

"Thank you again," I said and turned to him after we left the building.

He squinted down at me in a sleepy smile under the first rays of morning sun. "Thank you for coming with me."

He reached down and squeezed my hand in his briefly before letting it go with a wink. I was speechless as we got into our cars. His car rattled with music as he sped out of the parking lot and I followed him out, turning in the opposite direction, at a much more respectable speed and decibel level for five in the morning.

8

Tuesday was another night shift for me and Benjamin. I arrived a few minutes early, hoping to drink my coffee in peace, and check in with Donna about the latest gossip. But when I entered the staff door I was met with the sight of Oscar offering to boost Benjamin into the attic. Oscar was partially crouched with his arms down, hands clasped together like a stirrup. Benjamin was looking down at him and shaking his head.

"I'm not climbing you, Oscar," Benjamin said and looked up when I entered. "I'll go see if Greg has a ladder."

"What do we need from the attic?" I asked as I opened my locker.

"Painting supplies," Oscar and Benjamin echoed back.

Oscar handed me a painting smock and one of his old t-shirts. "It's time to paint the float for the parade."

"We have a float already?" I asked. "You built one?"

Oscar's eyes crinkled, and his mustache quivered in excitement. "I did!"

"When?" Benjamin asked, his brow furrowed. Benjamin was usually the person who did the building of Oscar's grand plans.

Not because he was skilled, but because he was a strong man and looked the part. Benjamin typically went along with it because it was something different to do. And I suspected he loved a good puzzle.

"I've been working on it for a while. I got the idea after last year's parade," Oscar said with a mischievous wiggle to his mustache.

Last year, we partnered with the local pediatricians' office, and we dressed as apples and the pediatricians acted like they were afraid of us. We had spooky music and a fog machine and lights shining like lightning flashes. It was a hit and only mildly traumatized the local children.

"Well, where is it?" I said and gestured for him to lead the way.

"We have to bring pieces of it in to paint and then we'll assemble it," Oscar explained as he had us follow him through the store to the parking lot across the street. His car was there with a rented moving trailer behind it. He used a key to unlock the trailer and opened it with a flourish.

Benjamin used the flashlight on his phone to illuminate the trailer. It was... pieces of wood?

Oscar beamed at us. Benjamin scratched his head, and I fought down a giggle.

"You're going to have to explain your vision," Benjamin said.

"I want it to look like an orchard, and that is all I will say until the parade," Oscar said and handed me his sketches.

Benjamin shone the light on the papers and leaned over my shoulder to look at them. Benjamin's chest brushed my shoulder. I had to work to not focus entirely on the contact. Oscar had spent time on these sketches. They were in color, with measurements, and specific instructions for how things should be painted.

"This is our assignment tonight?" Benjamin asked, his breath puffing over my ear and making me shiver.

"Yes, I would imagine one of you paints in the staff room and the other works up front. Benjamin, there is some scheduling to finish, too," Oscar replied as we loaded up our arms with pieces for the float.

Benjamin ended up finding the ladder and didn't need to climb on top of Oscar to get to the attic space above the staff room. He brought down the rest of the smocks, brushes, drop cloths, and a vast assortment of paints and stencils. Oscar and his father before him, had always made their own signs and store displays. It added to the charm of the store and has allowed many of the current and past employees to leave their mark.

Instead of painting in the staff room, I set up a space on one of the bagging areas to paint near the front in case Benjamin needed help with customers. And so that I could still be near to him. I put in my earbuds and listened to an audiobook while I painted an orchard backdrop to go behind the trees and against the cab of the truck. Painting while listening to a book in an empty store lulled me into a daze. I perched on my stool while I worked, facing away from the door while I worked on a part of the scene. When someone approached me, I felt them before I saw them. I had been so dazed that I didn't notice Benjamin come out of the office. He rested a hand on my shoulder, making me jump and go to stand up. I had tucked my foot behind the rung on the stool and the speed at which I tried to jump up caused me to go flying.

Strong arms wrapped around me, and my paintbrush clattered to the floor. Benjamin spun me in his arms, so I was chest to chest with him and I gasped. "Sorry!"

He smirked down at me and didn't let go. His eyes roamed over my face, and he looked like he wanted to say something before his eyes stopped on one of my earbuds. He let go of me to tug them out gently. I swallowed and bit my lip. He didn't step back.

"Did- did you need something?" I asked him, breathlessly.

"I wanted to see if you wanted to learn about the scheduling process," he replied. I was pressed against him firmly enough that I could feel the vibration of his voice in my chest. That vibration traveled south, and I clenched my thighs together.

"Scheduling?"

"Yeah, for when you have staff at your bookstore," he explained.

"Oh, right," I said and shook my head to kick start my brain cells.

Benjamin looked at my lips again and I wet them almost compulsively. His chest heaved and his eyes darkened in a way that I had never seen from him before. He looked like he was barely controlling something, and his jaw clenched. He reached for me again and had me pinned between the bagging area and his body, his hands gripping my painter's smock at my waist. I could feel the hard muscles of his body against me as we breathed and stared at each other. His body felt amazing on mine, and I wanted nothing more than to feel his lips on my heated skin.

The bell above the door chimed and Scoot, the owner of the

bar, came in. Benjamin stepped back with an exhale and turned to the door.

"Hey, Scoot," he said. "Donna close the bar?"

"Nah, she only comes in for dinner during the week," Scoot replied and picked up a basket. "Sorry to interrupt you two." He said and his eyes twinkled at us over his long, gray beard.

I blushed and turned back to my painting. "Let me know when you're done, Scoot."

"When he's gone, meet me in the office," Benjamin said and touched my elbow lightly.

With Benjamin back in the front office, I took a deep breath and sat on my stool. I only stared at the paints. My hands were shaking too much to be productive. I tidied my space while I waited for Scoot to finish his shopping.

Once Scoot was back in his car and the store was empty, I readied myself for being close to Benjamin again. I took off the painting smock and old t-shirt, so I was in my own clothes again. Smoothing down the front of my shirt, I went into the office.

"Scoot all set?" Benjamin asked and spun in the office chair to face me. He was reclined in the seat, a pen hanging from his lips.

"Mhm," I said and leaned against the desk.

"Alright, well come and resume your seat," he said casually and patted his leg.

I hesitated a moment before sitting on his lap the way I had done last shift. Straddling Benjamin's leg was exciting, and I loved being close to him, but I knew I should keep a boundary between us. When he rested a large, warm hand on my hip as he leaned to grab the mouse with his other, the idea of creating appropriate boundaries shattered and the fragments melted. Melted, much like my panties.

"Okay, teach me," I mumbled.

I heard him swallow over my shoulder. "Right, so we used to use a program that did it for us. But Donna is always fucking with Oscar with her schedule. Currently, she's not available before nine in the morning but she also says she can only start her shift on even numbers."

I snorted. "What did Oscar do?"

"I'm not sure of the entire story but it's something to do with the Apple Festival," Benjamin smiled. "But whenever she pulls this shit on Oscar, I'm actually the one who has to fuck around with the schedule and make it work. It's just easier to do manually than with a computer program. And it's better for you to see our system manually, since most small businesses do it this way."

I felt his thigh muscles bunch and then release as he rolled us forward to be closer to the keyboard. I became even more bodily aware of him. His leg between mine, pressed against the most private part of me, his thick arms around me, his long, tattooed fingers typing on the keyboard, and his even breath on my neck. Goosebumps arose on my skin at the awareness of him, and my core clenched around nothing.

"What does that sticky note say?" he asked me.

I leaned forward to look at the scribble on a blue Post It note on the monitor. As I leaned forward, my sensitive and impatient clit got the attention it craved, and a zing of pleasure shot up my spine. I blinked at the note as my pussy throbbed on his thigh. "Uh, it says James needs Thursday of next week off for a college interview," I rasped out after a moment of collecting my brain cells from my pelvic floor.

Benjamin grunted out his understanding as he opened up a spreadsheet of the current schedule and took James off the Thursday shift. I watched wordlessly as he changed the dates to the week we were scheduling for. "Once you have a pretty steady schedule figured out, it's mostly just changing for requests off and special events. Getting the main schedule right is tough, but the most satisfying when it clicks."

"I knew you liked puzzles," I said with a grin.

"Why? Because I look like a jigsaw puzzle?" he laughed. He clenched his hands into fists and then relaxed them, showing off his ink.

"No, I just had a feeling," I said, my mind not able to come up with any evidence to back it up other than that I was a creep.

"You're right, though. I do like puzzles. Especially girls who give mixed signals." His left hand returned to its place on my hip.

His touch made the warm, wet throb between my legs intensify. I needed to get this little lesson back under control.

"So, who takes James' Thursday shift?" I asked after a second.

"Um," he said with an exhale as he refocused on the computer. He clicked around for a moment before he figured it out. "On Thursday, James mostly stocks shelves with our new sale items, so nobody. Oscar will just have to cover breaks, and everyone can rotate the stocking. It's no big deal. See, you have to have a pretty intimate knowledge of your store and your staff when you schedule a small group like this."

"Intimate. Makes sense," I said and cleared my throat.

Benjamin's phone chimed with an alarm clock. He had an

alarm set to go off fifteen minutes before the end of shift so we could get the first shift registers ready and turn on the store's music and door heaters. I stood from his lap as he turned off the alarm. "I'll get started on opening stuff," I said and quickly left the almost suffocating lust cloud that had settled on the front office.

I had to shake my head to clear the fog as I turned on the store music. It was quiet enough that I heard the back staff door open as the five o'clock shift came in. It was a scramble to get my painting supplies cleared up while Benjamin opened registers and printed the new schedule for Oscar's approval. We didn't speak again until he followed me out the staff door after we both clocked out.

"Hey," he said to get my attention. He had already had my attention, but I hadn't been facing him as I walked across the staff lot.

"Yeah?" I said as I turned back to face him. I tried to remain cool, as if I wasn't literally holding my breath and waiting for him to stop me.

"Have a good day off. I'll see you Thursday," he said quietly and grabbed my hand. He held my fingers in his much larger hand and his thumb rubbed over my knuckles.

"You, too," I said, my voice sounding reedy.

"I'll bring us coffee for our next shift. We haven't bet on anything lately," he grinned.

I bit my lip. "I'll take one of your mochas."

"It will cost you," he said solemnly.

"If you remember, I don't use sexual favors as currency," I tried to joke. But my laugh got caught in my throat when I saw his eyes flash. It looked like his eyes had dilated in interest, but it was just after five in the morning and sunrise wasn't for another two hours. The dim lights of the parking lots did little for my vision, so it was possible I'd imagined it.

"I was going to ask for a wink," he clarified in his deep voice.

"You also know that I can't wink." I gave a breathy laugh now.

He smirked. "Fine, no mocha for you."

"Ugh," I gave a dramatic, exasperated groan and rolled my eyes. "Fine," I snapped and attempted to wink at him. But, as I had known, I failed and just awkwardly blinked at him.

He paused for a moment. "That was horrifying."

"Thank you. Do I get the mocha?"

"Yes. Your wink has earned you a mocha. And an exorcism," he said and gave my hand a last squeeze before stepping back.

"You asked for it," I giggled.

"That I did," he joked with a regretful tone.

I kicked some golden and orange leaves towards him. The big hickory tree behind the staff lot was one of the first to turn golden in the fall and drop its leaves.

He feigned a quick step towards me, and I squealed and turned and ran to my car. I turned back once I touched my door and saw him at his own car.

"Just wait until there are enough leaves on the ground to tackle you into, little one," he jokingly threatened.

"Ooh, I'm so scared," I sarcastically called back as I got into my car.

Once my door was shut, I chanced a look over at Benjamin and he was still outside of his car and shaking his head at me. One eyebrow cocked in challenge and a smirk on his lips.

9

It felt like my goal of opening the bookstore had taken a back seat. Working overnight, even just a few days a week, had me off kilter. It had been a few months of making sure I went to bed on time, that I correctly set my alarms, and my uniforms were clean. I had gone on a few book series binges as well during that time. It felt like there had been a cloud cover all summer that kept me from being completely conscious. Therefore, Wednesday afternoon had me sitting at my kitchen table making plans. I knew I needed books for a bookstore, and I had already been creating and adding to a list of authors and books I wanted to carry. It was extensive and exciting.

There were so many other things that I needed before I could open the doors of my store. One of those things being real estate. So, I scrolled through the listings of commercially zoned buildings that were for sale in town and the surrounding area. Nothing came up that suited my needs, and I was about to close my laptop when I saw that a French patisserie a few towns over had been remodeled and had some of its old equipment for sale. Looking through the listings, I saw they had an espresso machine for sale. It was a Jura Impressa, an older automatic model. Some research on the model and brand said that they meant it for home or small commercial use. I didn't need something huge and industrial. I wouldn't likely be making more than a few coffees an hour. It would be perfect for my store.

The French patisserie agreed to the price I had offered them as long as I picked it up. It was a chance of a lifetime. Or so it felt. But really, it was just good timing and a good deal. It would be a few hours drive round trip, so I loaded up a new audiobook, stopped at the bank for cash, and headed out on my road trip.

They assured me that the espresso machine still worked great; they had only remodeled and wanted an upgrade. I left with the machine strapped into the backseat like it was a child, a gigantic box of pastries, and a seventeen-hundred-dollar dent in my bank account. A small dent considering the fantastic condition of the machine. I couldn't wait to get it hooked up.

It was well past midnight when I finally returned home, so I only hooked it up and ran some cleaner through it. I had hoped to make a coffee Thursday morning before my shift at work, but my sleep schedule was so weird I had almost overslept.

I made it to work frustrated and in a bad mood. Luckily, Oscar had me in the staff room painting my entire shift. Nobody really spoke to me other than to compliment my mural of an orchard. I kept a scowl and my earbuds on the entire shift. I didn't see Benjamin much other than when he helped carry the finished pieces out to the trailer.

"You alright?" he asked me as we closed the door on the trailer. The chilly wind blew dried leaves across the surrounding pavement. The skipping scrape of them created a hushed white noise.

"Yeah," I sighed. "I was up late working on some stuff for my store."

"What was it?" he asked as he locked the trailer.

"I drove out to Emerald Hollow for an espresso machine, and I didn't get home until midnight," I explained and picked at some paint on my thumbnail.

"You what?" he sounded angry as he whirled towards me. Leaves crunched under his feet.

"I bought an espresso machine," I repeated and untied my painting smock.

"You drove hours away at night alone?" he asked in a scolding tone.

"Yeah, what of it?" I snapped. Benjamin's stiff anger had his jaw clenched and brow furrowed. He looked incredibly sexy, but I was in a bad mood. Bad enough that I mouthed off to him.

"Don't be a brat, you know why that's not alright," he snapped back.

I rolled my eyes and tried to walk past him. He grabbed my elbow and tugged me back to him. My hair whirled as I spun back to him, some of it getting caught in my eyelashes. I glared up at him.

"I was totally fine!" I gritted out, realizing that this lack of consistent sleep was not a cute look for my temperament.

"You got lucky," he said, his eyes still narrowed on me.

"I'm doing this business on my own, and sometimes-" I started, but he cut me off.

"If you need to get something across the state again, I'm

coming with you. I don't care if you're picking up shelving, boxes on boxes of books, or a single piece of paper. I'm coming with you," he insisted, his eyes softening on me as he spoke.

I swallowed and tried to step back, realizing I was being uncharacteristically bitchy, but couldn't because he still held my elbow in a tight grip. He stared at me for a moment, his eyes darting over my face, and a muscle twitched in his jaw.

"Okay," I whispered, conceding.

"Okay," he whispered back and used the hand not holding my arm to push my hair from my face. I blinked as the hair untangled from my eyelashes. He pinched my chin with his thumb and forefinger and his breath ghosted over my face. My breath caught in my chest as I realized how close we were to kissing. All he had to do was lean down. My eyes fluttered shut and my lips parted with a slow inhale as my heart rate kicked into high gear.

A door slammed somewhere behind me. I opened my eyes to see Benjamin barely two inches from my face, his eyes tracking someone behind us.

"Oscar!" a man, pharmacist Greg, was shouting. I heard the slam of the staff door opening and hitting the cement wall. "You cannot change our line up!" The door slammed shut.

Benjamin snorted a laugh and pulled away from me. He let go of my arm and the warmth of his nearness dissipated like a fog. "Oscar asked to have the parade order changed."

"Oh," I said. I couldn't have cared a speck less. My knees felt weak, and my core was liquid. Was Benjamin about to kiss me before we were interrupted?

"Yeah," Benjamin said awkwardly and rubbed the back of

his neck. "Our shift is over, so I'll see you tomorrow before the parade."

I nodded.

"I wonder what costumes go with an orchard theme?" Benjamin asked with a lopsided grin as he headed back to the store.

"Maybe we'll be trees," I said absently, hoping I didn't look as shaken as I felt.

"Goodnight, little one," Benjamin said with a wink as he clocked out.

"Goodnight," I said and gathered my things from my locker. I headed to my car with a shopping bag full of coffee beans and knees made of gelatin.

I was shaken out of my dazed state when I entered my apartment and saw the shining and clean espresso machine taking up most of my kitchen counter. I filled the water reservoir and filled the bean hopper and switched the machine on. The manual was easily found online, and I had studied it during my break at work. It worked beautifully as it pulled two perfect espresso shots into one of my coffee mugs. I would have to buy the accessories that went with the machine, but in the meantime, I had some amazing coffee at home. I frothed some milk after watching a tutorial online and made myself a latte. It was amazing.

I spent the rest of the evening creating different flavored syrups for my menu. Vanilla, cinnamon, caramel, almond, and mint. I melted down some dark chocolate and made a mocha with a caramel drizzle. It was exactly what Benjamin liked. I sent him a quick text and told him to meet me at the gazebo in town. Wired on caffeine and excitement and creative energy, I hadn't even looked at the time. I threw on my thrifted plaid peacoat over my pajamas and hopped in my car, travel mug and a book in hand. I had found a great thriller novel that I thought he would like. It had the same level of taboo spice that I knew had shocked him in the last book I'd given him.

Pulling up to the gazebo, I realized that the only lights in town were for Oscar's store and the twinkling lights around the gazebo. Since we weren't there, another team was working the overnight shift. Oscar had to hire a few people specifically for overnights since Benjamin and I were the only established employees who were willing to continue to do it. It wasn't until I parked and went to stand under the lights of the gazebo that I realized it was late. I hadn't even looked at the time and my phone was still in my car.

I was about to go check the time when Benjamin's car came speeding up to the gazebo. He stopped his car in the street since nobody was out driving but us. He jumped out of the car and ran around it to leap up the gazebo stairs in two strides. Benjamin approached me quickly, but I had time to register that he was wearing unbuttoned jeans pulled up over black boxers that bunched around his hips, a white tank top, an open leather jacket, untied black motorcycle boots, and a crazed expression. His expression and speed shocked me, so I stepped back.

"What's wrong? What happened? Are you okay?" he asked, coming up short.

"Nothing, I'm fine. Um, I made you a coffee," I said, feeling dumb.

"Layla... it's two in the morning," he said incredulously and looked me up and down like I did not convince him there wasn't something wrong.

"Oh," I said and looked down, definitely feeling dumb now.

He held out his hand.

I hesitated.

"This better be the best damn coffee if it got me out of bed at two in the morning," he said, looking down his nose at me as he stepped closer. He had a small smirk on his lips as he wrapped his hand around mine on the mug.

He opened the mug and took a sip. He hummed and took another sip.

"I made the chocolate sauce and the caramel drizzle," I said in a small voice.

"You did?" he asked as he took another long sip.

I nodded.

"You did good, little one," he said and sat on the bench along the gazebo wall.

"Thank you," I said and sat next to him. I set the book between us on the bench. "I brought you a book that I think you'd like."

"Another kinky one?" he asked.

I blushed and nodded. "It's also a thriller."

"More knife play?" he asked.

"No, is that your request?" I giggled.

"I learned something with that last book. Something about myself," he chuckled.

"I'll keep that in mind."

He looked at me.

"For future book recommendations," I clarified.

He hummed and took another sip of his coffee.

"You don't have to drink it if it's bad. Or if you don't think you'll be able to sleep tonight," I said and looked out at the still and quiet town.

"It's wonderful, Layla," he said and sat the mug down next to the book. "You did a good job."

I blushed at his praise.

"You'll have a great selection at your store, I'm sure of it," he said and leaned back on the bench.

We were silent for a few moments. He had come racing into town at a moment's notice for me. I had summoned him at two in the morning for what, a coffee and a book?

"Were you sleeping when I texted you?" I asked him.

"Yeah," he said and yawned. "I was."

"Oh," I considered. "Then why did you come?"

"Honestly? I thought you- well, I thought you were calling me for something else," he chuckled.

"Like there was a problem at Oscar's or something?" I asked.

"No, like a booty call," he explained, and looked down at me with a shy grin.

"Oh my god," I groaned and put my face in my hands. My entire body cringed with embarrassment.

Benjamin chuckled and patted my back.

"But you came." I sat back up and spoke. He had thought I was calling him for sex, and he actually drove to meet me in the middle of the night.

"Not yet, I didn't," he said with a naughty smirk.

I opened my mouth to tell him he was being vulgar when lights flashed behind us on the street. I jumped and Benjamin whirled around.

"Everything alright over here?" an authoritative voice rang out.

"Hey Officer Dan," Benjamin greeted and stood up.

"Hey Ben, I thought that was your car in the street," Officer Dan said, his voice losing some of the harshness.

"Sorry, I'll move it," Benjamin said and started towards his car, holding his book and the travel mug. "We were just leaving, anyway."

Officer Dan looked at me as I descended the gazebo steps. His hands were on his hips and his stance suggested he had been ready for a fight. I smiled shyly at him.

"Everything alright, Layla?" Officer Dan was the New Cop on the force despite having been there since I was in high school. He was only a handful of years older than me and had joined the police academy as soon as he could.

"Yeah, just a little mental breakdown," Benjamin said and winked at me.

Officer Dan's posture relaxed for a second before he rushed into his line of questioning. "Do you want to hurt yourself or others? Are you currently under the influence of any subst-"

"I don't think you're supposed to read out the pink slip criteria like that." Benjamin scrunched his face in confusion. "But no, it's not like that."

"I'm fine, Officer Dan," I said confidently. "I just wanted to talk to a friend."

"Well, okay then," he said. "Ben, please move your car. If I come around the block and you're still parked there, I'll have to issue a citation."

Benjamin saluted him as he walked back to his cruiser.

Once Officer Dan was back in his car and pulling away, I turned to Benjamin. "I'm sorry to wake you up and make you come."

"Or not come," Benjamin amended.

"Or not," I agreed with a giggle.

"Thank you for the book and the coffee, little one," he said and walked towards his car.

"Officer Dan called you Ben. Has that been an option this whole time?" I called to him.

Benjamin tilted his head back with a laugh. His genuine laugh. "The only people who call me Benjamin are the people at Oscar's. I applied with my full name and Oscar introduced me with it and by then I was in too deep. My family calls me Benji, and my friends call me Ben."

"Can I call you Ben?" I asked.

He considered me over the hood of his car for a moment. "No, I like when you say my name. Goodnight, little one. I'm waiting to watch you leave."

Saying nothing back, I got into my car and drove home in silence. Embarrassment and arousal warred for dominance over the warmth of my body. Once home, I ignored the mess in my kitchen and crashed into bed. I would be awake again in just a few hours for a double shift. It was parade day.

10

Friday was sure to be a long day with a full shift ending in the parade and start of the Apple Festival. Our town prided itself on our apple harvest every year, and it had been a huge celebration for as long as our town had been around. It was a fun event but would make for an exhausting day to have after being awake until almost three in the morning. I filled two of my travel mugs with a vanilla latte with extra espresso to get me moving this morning. Benjamin texted me with the demand for coffee as I was yawning and just about to leave. I smiled and filled my remaining two travel mugs with mochas with extra espresso and caramel drizzle. By the time I finished and arrived at work, Benjamin was already there, leaning his forehead against his locker, his apron hanging loosely in his hand.

"Benji, I made you coffee," I teased.

"Don't," he muttered in a sleepy gruff voice.

I giggled. "Sorry, I couldn't help it. You're named after a dog."

"Is there extra espresso in it?" he changed the topic.

"There is," I answered and held out the mugs that were his. "I made two for you."

He rolled his head on the locker to look at me, a sleepy eyebrow quirked. When his eyes fell on the two travel mugs, he pushed away from the metal and snatched the mugs from my hand. I laughed at his enthusiasm. He opened one and took a long swallow. He hummed in appreciation and looked at me mischievously. "Not as good as a two a.m. booty call. But it'll do."

"What's this about a booty call?" Donna's voice rasped from inside Oscar's office. She came around the corner, bundles of fabric in her hands and an excited look on her face.

"Nothing," Benjamin and I said simultaneously.

"Liars," she cackled. "Who called who?"

"Nobody called anybody," we echoed again and then shared a look and clinked our mugs together in cheers.

"You two spend too much time together for people who aren't fu-"

"That's nice, Donna. We appreciate your concern. See you out front," I interrupted her loudly.

She gave a sly grin and went through the swinging doors to the store.

"Between her and Officer Dan, expect to hear about your anticlimactic booty call from at least three customers before noon," Benjamin said and drained the rest of his first mug.

"How would they know it was anticlimactic?" I laughed.

"Officer Dan wasn't called for a noise complaint," Benjamin said and waggled his eyebrows at me. He picked up the second mug. It was pastel pink with yellow sunflowers on it and my name in fancy script. It had been a gift a few years back. There was just something about a muscled, tattooed, Dark Romance Book Character holding dainty and floral items that grabbed my attention. I had always loved the books where the main male character was only soft for his girl. While Benjamin was a kind soul, seeing him drinking out of my bedazzled and flowery mug gave me the same feelings as those books. It was the juxtaposition for my sake that caused my heart to squeeze and my panties to dampen. Panties that were white with dainty little pink roses on them with a white lace trim. Panties that would look fantastic gripped in Benjamin's tattooed fist.

"Oh, ha ha," I said breathlessly and delayed.

"Well, little one, let's get to work," Benjamin said and led us through to the store.

The store was buzzing with activity. Customers were doing their shopping and Oscar was animatedly talking to a group of employees. Everyone fell quiet as we approached, and my stomach sank. I glared at Donna who shook her head to assure me this wasn't about what she overheard in the staff room. My stomach still didn't unclench. Benjamin elbowed me.

"Alright, what's the costume?" Benjamin said in a conciliatory tone.

A few people snorted or chuckled.

"I'm not giving out costumes until just before the parade," Oscar replied, and his mustache twitched with amusement.

"Nuh-uh," Benjamin said, likely also noting the mustache. "I need to know if I have to wax."

"That's what I'm sayin'!" Donna exclaimed in agreement.

"It's a secret, and it's a very conservative costume," Oscar said with a blush at all the wax-talk. "No need for- uh- waxing."

Benjamin hummed to say he was still suspicious, and Oscar threw his hands in the air.

"We were just discussing who was going to set up the float," Donna said, having mercy for Oscar's nerves.

"Oh, I'll help you with that," Benjamin offered Oscar, who nodded.

"Layla, you'll be ringing this morning. We want the customers to see you most of the day before the parade," Donna added.

"Why? Are we scaring children again?" I asked. A couple of my coworkers giggled at the memory.

"No, but you're going to look different this evening," Oscar said with another amused mustache wiggle.

Nothing more was said on the topic, and Oscar sent me to the register while Benjamin was on construction duty. It was a busy day in the store with people in and out doing their weekend shopping and preparing for the festival. I didn't even see him on my lunch break, but a chai tea latte with a shot of espresso was delivered by a confused James early in the afternoon. "Benjamin said to give this to you," he said with a shrug before scurrying off to tell his girlfriend that the coffee wasn't from him.

When the store closed early, and technically for the first time since early summer, the entire staff seemed to take a deep breath before looking at Oscar. Oscar, who was grinning at us with a wiggling mustache, was in his element. This event was his personal Superbowl. And because of his joyful excitement, nobody let him down, and everybody took part with enthusiasm in all of his antics. We may have rolled our eyes behind his back, but we all loved seeing Oscar happy.

"Everyone, I'd like to introduce you all to... drumroll please...." We obliged him. "Mr. and Mrs. Johnny Appleseed!"

Everyone cheered, including me and Benjamin, before we

realized Oscar was pointing to us. I hadn't realized Benjamin was standing directly next to me until I looked to see who else Oscar was pointing to.

"Oh, wait, what?" I asked.

"You and Benjamin are Mr. and Mrs. Appleseed on the float this year!" Oscar explained.

"That's so great!" Benjamin said with fake enthusiasm. I elbowed him in the ribs.

And seconds after that, everyone burst into action. Oscar shouted orders, more people arrived, and everyone was talking and moving. They ushered Benjamin and me into the staff room and handed us our costumes. Donna slammed a huge make-up case on the table.

I was pushed into Oscar's office with Donna while Benjamin went into the staff bathroom. Donna helped me lace up a gold corset over a cream and gold flowered dress. A huge, powdered wig was placed on my head with a fall leaf crown. It was incredibly historically inaccurate. I was pretty sure that not only did Johnny Appleseed not come through this part of the state, but he didn't marry, and he wore ragged clothes and no shoes. If he had a wife, it wasn't likely she'd wear this type of clothing. I almost looked like I belonged on Marie Antoinette's court in late 1700's France. The corset pushed my breasts until they were almost obscene and about to burst out of the dress. I could barely breathe, and I was thankful that my role in the parade was standing and waving.

Once I finished dressing, it was time to leave. Benjamin and I were both shoved into the back of Donna's old Chevy Blazer. It smelled like stale cigarette smoke, dog fur, and Love

Spell perfume from Victoria's Secret. Benjamin knocked his shoulder into mine. "Hey there Marie Antoinette," he chuckled. "Nice tits."

"I know, right?" I laughed. "Johnny Appleseed didn't even get married, let alone to a member of the French court."

"Really?" he asked.

I bent down and dug through my skirts to find where I'd tucked my phone into my thigh-high stockings. I pulled it out and did a quick Google search. Benjamin was silent as I showed him the screen. "See?"

"I do. But uh, where was your phone?" he asked, his expression a mixture of shock, fear, and interest.

"Ew, stop. It was in my stocking," I said and slapped his arm. "Actually, can you hold it while we're on the float? Do you have pockets?"

Benjamin was wearing gray, high-waisted and narrow trousers that clung to his muscular legs and showcased his bulge in a rather flattering but almost pornographic way. He had a golden vest with an apple pattern, a long black coat, and a red ascot around his neck. In his hand was a saucepan. "What are you wearing?" I asked with a laugh.

"Not a clue other than some really tight pants," Benjamin said and huffed a laugh.

"Johnny Appleseed was poor. He wore rags. Apparently we'd do anything for Oscar," I said.

"Apparently," he grumbled as Donna got into the driver's seat, shouting at Oscar who was getting into someone else's car.

She started the car and took off to the start of the parade. We didn't talk while she drove, not wanting to distract her. The sidewalks were lined and crowded with people. Children were waving streamers in fall colors and parents talked around coolers of beer. Officer Dan and a few other cops were directing us to a parking lot at the start of the historic town center and to Oscar's borrowed Ford Truck with a flatbed trailer decorated with all of my artwork and what looked like two small apple trees in front of a platform. The trailer was decorated bigger than we've ever done for the parade. It had two levels with railings all around it and two real trees in pots. I was impressed.

"She's a beaut," Benjamin said proudly as we parked. Oscar was already out of James' car and was practically sprinting to do a last check of the float. My dress prevented me from getting out on my own and Donna pulled me out while Benjamin was called away by a frantic Oscar. Donna fluffed out my dress skirts and Oscar helped me onto the trailer, and then Benjamin was there to help me onto the smaller, higher platform. His hand was warm in mine as he looked down at me with a smile on his face.

Once we were situated on the float, Oscar and Donna ran off to give directions to the rest of the staff who were to be handing out candied apples, toys, and sale flyers to the people lining the streets. There was a flurry of loud activity around us and Benjamin and I just watched, removed from it all. James came over to us with big, metal tankards of apple cider. He wished us luck and looked us over in our costumes like we were crazy before leaving to go back to his girlfriend. Everyone else was wearing the fall festival themed t-shirts with the name of Oscar's store on the front and fall leaf necklaces and crowns. I took a sip of the cool, sweet cider. Benjamin nudged me and I looked up at him. He still had a grin on his face, but he now had the saucepan on his head like a hat. I had forgotten about that part of the costume and a few giggles escaped at the sight of him.

"Don't laugh at the guy who brought this," he said and produced a silver flask with a flourish from his coat pocket. "I figured we would need some liquid reinforcements."

I held out my tankard and looked around to see if anyone was watching as he tipped a good portion of alcohol into my cider. "What is it?"

"Spiced rum," he replied quietly to avoid notice. He poured some into his own tankard that I held for him before tucking the flask back into his coat.

We both clanked them together as more people arrived to get on the float. We maintained eye contact as we took long drinks of the now spiced cider. His brown eyes were warm and crinkled at the corners in a smile. It felt like we were on a team together. It was us, together, in front of the world. Even though it was just a silly parade in our tiny town, it felt... meaningful. We had a secret now, too. The spiced cider warmed me all the way to my belly and the closeness with Benjamin warmed me further down. The trailer rocked as people got on the lower level and I broke eye contact to investigate a less familiar giggle.

"Oh my god," I said in a choked voice. Benjamin sputtered while drinking his cider and had to turn away to cough it out of his lungs, wiping his eyes and mouth with his coat sleeve.

Three of the girls from Edible Entertainment, the topless waitresses, stood looking up at us. They were not, in fact, topless, but dressed in apple costumes. One red, one yellow, and one green. Their faces and arms stuck out of the padded material and if nobody looked further down, they looked like small children in the obligatory pumpkin Halloween costume. If someone looked further down, they would see long legs in black fishnet tights ending in color coordinating stiletto heels. One girl turned around to listen to a direction given by Oscar and I saw they painted her butt cheeks to be the bottom part of the apple where the costume ended in a thong. I almost spat out my cider. Next to me, Benjamin fared no better.

"Hello, ladies," Benjamin coughed out finally. "So nice to see you again."

"You know we can't turn down an Oscar event," Lily, one waitress, said. She was the red apple, and her lipstick also matched.

"Did he pick out the costumes?" I asked, trying not to laugh.

Next to me, Benjamin took another long swallow of his drink.

Lily smiled. "He did, actually."

"Who- uh- who painted you?" Benjamin asked, clearly trying not to laugh as well.

"We painted each other," Betsy, the green apple, replied. She made green lipstick look sexy. I would have looked like I belonged on a set for Wizard of Oz. "But you can help us wash it off later," she said with a wink at Benjamin.

"Ah, sorry, I'm signed up for booth duty. Can't, uh, help with booty duty," Benjamin said, and his blush crept up his cheeks in splotches. His ascot covered his tattooed neck and the red of the silky material matched his face.

"Too bad," Betsy said just as the yellow apple, Anna, turned to relay their instructions.

James and Oscar were frantically arguing about a Bluetooth speaker that was being set up at the foot of the float and I looked around to see the other floats and groups filing out of the parking lot. There was the high school marching band and a few of the sports teams, a children's baton and dance group, a few kids dressed in karate uniforms spastically wielding foam nunchaku, the local boy and girl scout groups, a senior citizen dance group, and the local elected officials all on foot. While the pediatricians, dentists, Greg the pharmacist, the library, a few local lawyers, a pizza shop, the animal shelter, and Oscar's store all had floats. We were one of the last floats to leave, and the beginning twangs of bluegrass music blared out of the speaker as we jolted into motion. Oscar drove the decorated red truck carefully, watching us all closely as he maneuvered down the curb.

Benjamin caged me in against the railing, his warmth at my back, as we plopped off the curb. "Drink up, little one. This is working out to be a fever dream of an event."

I took a long drink of my cider and shook my head in disbelief. The three sexy apples twirled seductively to the bluegrass music while Benjamin and I waved at the people at the start of the parade route. This was a surreal experience.

"This is our life right now," I said to Benjamin as a group of adults held up their own drinks in a cheers-salute to us on the float. We did it in return.

"If you would have told me on my first day at Oscar's I would have... honestly believed you and still stuck around. This is awesome. How would we even explain this to anyone? Yeah, one time I pretended to be fucking Johnny Appleseed in a parade with a fucking saucepan on my head, with three topless waitresses dressed as bottomless apples and stripper dancing to fucking bluegrass. Nobody would believe this. Anna is twerking while dressed as a yellow delicious apple and I'm barefoot and wearing fancy Victorian clothes," Benjamin said, his eyes alight.

I looked down at his feet. He had the bones of his skeleton tattooed on the top of his bare feet. "I wondered what that smell was," I said sarcastically.

"No way," he said with an embarrassed look. "My feet aren't usually smelly, but I got nervous, so I washed them in the staff bathroom sink before we left. Are they really that bad?"

I burst out laughing. He didn't smell; I had only been kidding. When I told him as much, he laughed with me. And when green apple Betsy and red apple Lily began grinding on each other to banjo music, our laughter grew to hysterics. Benjamin's genuine laugh had no choice but to come out in loud, lilting breaths until we were both wheezing and silent laughing with eyes streaming. We clutched each other as our laughter continued, sloshing our cider about as we raised our tankards in salute with the adults on the sidewalks. When our laughter had died down to fits of giggles, I was still in Benjamin's arms. It was a cool evening, and it felt good being wrapped in his embrace. I leaned into him and smiled up at him. My tankard was empty now, and the spiced rum left a buzzed feeling in my head. He smiled down at me, his cheeks flushed red with his own buzz.

"Mr. Appleseed, I believe you've gotten me tipsy," I said with a breathless giggle and fanned my heated face.

"Oh, Mrs. Appleseed, that was the point," he said in a low voice.

Under all of my skirts and layers, I felt a pressure against my ass. "Are you groping me?" I asked Benjamin, my mouth falling open.

"I've been trying to grope you this whole time, are you just now feeling it? How many layers are you wearing?" Benjamin asked.

"Way too many," I laughed. "Why are you trying to grope me? This is a family event!"

"We're supposed to be married. Don't husbands grab their wives' ass? I feel like that's the whole point," he said and groped me again.

"Stop," I laughed and batted his hands away before leaning over and giving his ass a squeeze. It was a good handful, and I realized mid squeeze I had my hands on Benjamin's ass cheeks. The spiced rum had gone straight to my head after a long, exhausting day. Or, rather, straight between my legs, if I was honest. I looked up at him, suddenly shocked by my own audacity. He only grinned down at me with a sly expression.

The parade itself wasn't very long but ended at the fairgrounds and a photoshoot opportunity. While the Edible Entertainment girls fielded all the leering men, Benjamin and I had our pictures taken with multiple children and families. Donna was our dedicated photographer and director and kept the line moving quickly.

I didn't get the chance to talk with Benjamin again before someone ushered him away to man the booth while I was sent to walk around with candied apples for the children at the fair. It was late when we were dismissed from our shift and the fair closed. Donna had somehow had her truck dropped off at the fairgrounds and was the one to drive me and Benjamin back to Oscar's. We were silent again on the drive back, but this time because of exhaustion and not apprehension. I leaned my head on his shoulder until my big wig tickled his nose and he pushed me away with a chuckle.

Back at the store, Donna helped me out of my enormous dress, and I took off the wig. She was quiet with me as we packed everything up. Benjamin came out of the staff bathroom, yawning, and carrying his costume. Donna helped him package the costume to return to the rental place tomorrow. We were all silent as we grabbed our keys and left the store. Donna waved to us half heartedly as she got into her truck and Benjamin ruffled my hair before we separated and got into our cars.

I leaned back in my seat for a moment, willing my eyes to remain open. The drive home was quiet, and I slowly made my way into my apartment. I didn't even wash off the costume makeup or brush out my hair before collapsing into my bed. Tomorrow was another day at the festival, though only a five-hour shift.

Another day of wondering what Benjamin thought of me and stressing about how I was presenting myself to him. Another day feeling like I couldn't breathe around him. Another day wanting nothing more than to fall into his arms. I sighed as I fell asleep, thinking of how his arms felt around me during the parade, the pressure of him gripping my ass, and the sly smirk on his face when I had returned the favor.

11

Saturday's shifts were split for everyone between the festival and the store. I spent my morning in the store while Benjamin's morning shift was at the festival, and we switched in the afternoon. I was with Donna for both parts, and we were chattier than we had been last night. She told me all the local gossip and drama that happened at Scoot's bar and about everyone who had adopted from her corgi rescue. I had never thought a bunch of fifty-plus year-old people could get into so much trouble and drama. It was like watching reality TV. I sipped some fresh lemonade and listened intently to her hushed stories after people left our booth and wondered if I'd get as much drama and action at my bookstore.

Our store was passing out candied apples and sale flyers again, so a few employees were walking around the festival with trays and handfuls. At the booth we sold bottled water, bottled cider, and a few baked items with the proceeds going to Donna's corgi rescue. Pictures of Oscar's three corgis in costumes matching events at the store were plastered all over the back of the booth.

Oscar was somewhere pushing his dogs around in a wagon with his two giggling granddaughters.

I had missed seeing Benjamin. We had only high-fived in passing as I took over for him at the booth. When James and his girlfriend arrived for their evening shift in the booth, Donna and I left in search of some good and greasy fair food. I located some fried vegetables, more lemonade, and a huge apple fritter and left the festival. I stopped back at the store to grab my things and clock out, and left the apple fritter in Benjamin's locker. He was up front in the store, finishing up his shift, so I knew he would get it before he left. Upon opening my locker, I saw another huge apple fritter drizzled with caramel waiting for me. A note in Benjamin's neat and slanting handwriting said "To Mrs. Appleseed" was in front of it. I pocketed the note with a giddy feeling in my chest and grabbed a piece of paper from Oscar's office. I wrote a note for Benjamin that said, "Apparently Mr. and Mrs. Appleseed are meant to be together" before I chickened out and threw it away. Quickly, I wrote a second note that said, "Dear Mr. Appleseed, you're the apple of my eye" and left it with his dessert in his locker.

Instead of sticking around, I hurried out of the store before he came to clock out. I wondered if he realized this meant we had both been thinking about each other during the day apart. And I wondered if he was thinking about me in the same way. I left the parking lot with a smile on my face and anticipated hearing from him. It wasn't until I was home, showered, and eating my fried veggies while reading a book that my phone chimed. I picked it up quickly to see a picture of Benjamin, presumably at home, shirtless and taking a huge bite of apple fritter. My body felt warm as I stared at the picture. His entire chest was tattooed with black ink, and I could see just the top of his abs in the picture. He turned his head enough that I could only see one corner of his mouth curved up in a smile as he bit into the apple fritter. His eyes were crinkled in a smile. I stared long enough at the picture to notice his hair was also wet from a shower, he had a black leather couch, and gray walls in his living room.

Inspired, I picked up my apple fritter from the kitchen, my book, and phone and ran to my bedroom. I took my hair down from my messy bun, applied some tinted lip balm and mascara, and flopped on the bed. I laid the book open on the bed in front of me as if I had been lying in bed while reading. I was wearing an old pink tank top, and a knitted gray cardigan. To look sexy, I moved my boobs so they looked like they were almost falling out of my tank top, slid one shoulder out of the cardigan and posed to take a bite out of the apple fritter in the soft light of my bedroom. It felt naughty and almost like I was sending him naked pictures, but there was nothing blatantly inappropriate about the picture. I looked it over before I sent it. I had mirrored his smile around the bite of fritter and was wearing more clothes than he was in his selfie, so I felt confident when I pressed send.

His response was almost immediate. "Looking forward to seeing you tomorrow night. X."

I stared at his message. My heart pounded in my chest. I typed out a quick reply and sent it before I could chicken out again. "Same. Xx." I had to throw my phone across the room and scream into my pillow a few times before I could calm down. I needed to tell him tomorrow. I needed to tell him how I felt about him.

Sunday was an overnight shift, and it was already fully dark when I arrived at Oscar's. I was used to the store feeling sleepy and still. I welcomed the quiet. Tonight, there were still a bunch of customers in the store when I got there, and Benjamin and I were busy for a few hours. We could do little other than smile in greeting before we both worked in check out. It was near midnight before the customers slowed to the trickle of occasional people coming in for a few last-minute items. It seemed like everyone had spent the weekend at the festival and realized Sunday evening that they had nothing in the house for the week ahead. After the customers slowed, I worked a few hours on restocking the shelves and Benjamin stayed up front and worked on something in the office.

A crackling sound came over the store's intercom before Benjamin's voice announced "Mrs. Appleseed, please come to the front office. Mrs. Appleseed, to the front office."

I smiled and headed up front, having just finished restocking the dairy. I entered the office to see Benjamin sitting at the desk, his chair turned so I could reclaim my seat on his lap like the last few times he'd shown me something. He looked up and said, "Hey, let's work on some inventory."

"How is that different from ordering?" I asked as I sat on his lap, straddling his left thigh.

"This is how we run reports to see what our biggest sellers were this week to determine if we need more of something," he said and turned us towards the computer. "See, we sold more apples than usual. No surprise there, but we will need to consider that for our ordering. Oh, and canned pumpkin. We sold out."

"Hm," I said. I was sitting on his lap again. His strong thigh pressed against my core, and I had a hard time not concentrating on the sensation. He moved his foot and the angle of his leg changed, tipping me forward just the slightest bit. Just enough to put pressure on my clit. I fought to keep my breathing regular as I listened to his explanation of how the report was run. The butterflies in my core pounded an erratic rhythm.

He stopped talking and leaned forward in his seat. I looked over my shoulder at him, expecting to see him staring at the screen, but he was looking at me. His hands slid to cover my thighs with a light squeeze. "You know I can feel that, right?"

My stomach dropped to the floor, and shame filled me. "What?" I gasped with wide eyes and a gaping mouth.

"I can feel you clenching around my thigh," he said, his voice low and gravelly.

"Cl- clenching?" I asked and gave a small shake of my head, trying to play dumb.

He let out a breathy laugh and it blew against my overheated neck. "Yeah, little one. It's like you're trying to pull me into you. Trying to fill yourself with me. Is that what your naughty pussy is trying to tell me?"

I gasped in shock and pleasure. He leaned over further, and his lips caught mine. It felt like my entire body had been electrified when our lips met. His kiss was not soft, it was demanding and hot. His lips were smooth and soft, more pillowy than I'd thought they'd be. When I returned the kiss after a moment of shock, he groaned against my mouth. His hands moved from my thighs to my waist, and he lifted me off of him. I turned around, unsteady on my feet, and he forcefully pulled me back down onto his lap. I was straddling his hips now, our cores pressed together on the old office chair. My face was even with his and I looked into his warm brown eyes, now almost black with desire. I had planned on telling him today that I had feelings for him, and I guessed this worked just as well.

He pulled me closer, his fingers in my belt loops, so my jean covered pussy was tight against his bulge. I could feel just how much he had appreciated our kiss. He was hard and hot and huge beneath me. I rocked into him without thinking, and he moaned and kissed me again. His lips and tongue and teeth were demanding and devouring. I felt entirely consumed by him and we were only kissing. His grip on my ass was rough as he rolled my hips against his. Heat roiled through my veins, and I thought I would catch fire. I gasped again against his mouth at the sensation.

"Oh yeah? You like that? Is that greedy little pussy happy now?" Benjamin groaned against my skin as he kissed and sucked a line down my neck. "Or does she need more?"

"More," I moaned and gripped his curly blonde hair as he kissed across my collarbone. I could feel the fuse lit for an orgasm and I was desperately trying to meet it. Right here in his lap in the office at Oscar's- and I didn't care one bit. I felt wild with the desperation and desire for him.

"Hmm," he hummed against my skin. His hands gripped my ass almost painfully. "You didn't say the magic word."

"Please," I begged and rocked against him. "Please." I didn't recognize my voice. It was strained and whimpering and full of lust.

"If I put my hand in your pants, how wet would I find you?" he asked in that gravelly voice.

"Very," I said, desperation in my voice as I climbed closer and closer to climax.

He moaned, his head tipped back and eyes fluttering as he bit his lip. "I can't wait to feel that pussy around my cock. I want to feel you clenching and dripping."

I was so close, and it seemed like he was, too. We were barely more than dry humping, and I was about to come undone. His grip on my ass tightened painfully and his thrusts against me were harder and less controlled. His moan was more eager than before, and he bit down on my lip. The moisture in my panties made it harder to get the friction I needed, and I ground down even harder against him.

The bell above the front door chimed and Benjamin broke away to look up at the security feed above my head. His brow furrowed, but he didn't stop his movement. "We can finish if we're quiet," he said breathlessly.

We had only ground against each other a few more times before there was a different chime and Benjamin looked back up at the security feeds. "Oh shit," he said and pushed me back a few inches. "That's the morning crew coming in."

"Oh no," I said and scrambled off of him and looked at the clock. It was already five.

I heard voices as they approached the front office. I attempted to straighten my clothes. He was doing the same, standing up from the office chair.

"Fuck fuck fuck fuck," he chanted as he adjusted himself in his pants. I felt bad for his situation but also prideful because *I* did that.

Benjamin jumped back into the seat and rolled up to the

desk all the way and woke up the computer screen. "See, we need to order more canned pumpkin. But we knew that already from previous year trends. As the weather gets cooler- oh, hey guys," Benjamin said casually as our replacements came in. I didn't know these people very well, as Oscar had recently hired them. One was a mom whose kids had recently started high school and could get themselves on the bus and the other was a man who had retired from teaching music and had gotten bored and wanted another job. They were nice enough, but I hadn't worked or talked to them much this summer.

My heart rate slowed and the pulsing need between my legs subsided as I gave a quick rundown of the evening to them in terms of what I had cleaned and restocked. It had been a rather busy evening before I started restocking, and bread was to be shelved when it got delivered in a few hours. By the time I was putting my apron in my locker and grabbing my keys to leave, the desperation for Benjamin had faded. He stood next to me as I clocked out.

"I need to get home to sleep. I'm helping my parents paint their kitchen later this afternoon. Otherwise, I'd have you come with me," he whispered as he clocked out.

I shook my head. "It's okay. I actually have a meeting with a company that sells shelving for stores. I'm getting quotes on bookshelves and tables."

"Really? Do you have a location yet?" he asked brightly as we walked out the back door.

"No, not yet. But I really want to know what I'd be looking at for the cost of shelving and seating. I feel like I'm so unprepared for when I actually get a space, you know?" I said as we approached our cars.

"I get it. I actually already have most of the equipment for a tattoo shop in the shed at my parents' house," he said and rubbed his hand over the back of his neck.

I opened the door to my car and looked up at him. "I'll um, see you tomorrow then."

He smiled at me and leaned down to place a sweet kiss on my lips. This kiss had less of the fire from before, but was just as perfect. I sighed into the kiss, and I felt him smile against my lips. "See you tomorrow, little one."

I got into my car with shaky knees and trembling hands. I breathed for a few moments as my car heated up before I gathered the nerve to go home and sleep. Alone.

12

Monday had felt excruciatingly long. After I left work at five in the morning, I went home and tried to take a few hours of a nap before my meeting. The attempt at a nap proved to be futile as I had remained awake thinking about the heated kisses I had shared with Benjamin. Remembering his hands on my body and his lips on my skin kept me wide awake and unsatisfied. I gave up on napping and took a long, self-indulgent bath instead. The more I remained unoccupied by a task, the more my body wound up with tension and unresolved lust. By the time I left for my afternoon meeting, I felt tightly wound and frantic. But I had smoothed my hair, worn professional makeup, and dressed in a gray blazer and black skirt. Outwardly, I presented as a put together and profitable business woman. Internally, I was a jumble of tension and lust.

The meeting with the business furniture supplier was about an hour of a drive from my apartment. I remembered Benjamin's warning to take him with me the next time I had to go far from home, but I shook it off. I was a grown woman and could do things on my own without a chaperone. However, I would *not* be capable of keeping my hands off of him the next time I saw him, and I knew it. I was in the meeting for about two hours looking at their design packages for different stores and learning about their ordering process. This company had design packages all the way from table and chair sets to entire store makeovers including paint and fixtures. I could be as hands on or as hands off as I could afford or wanted. Their business model was inviting, and I brought home multiple design manuals and ideas for what my store could look like. I just... needed a store.

I was just getting home with spicy Thai takeout when I got a text from Benjamin. Setting my plastic bag of delicious smelling food on the counter, I opened it to see another picture message. I swallowed. He was sweaty, flecked with paint, with his head tilted back like he was sighing with exhaustion, and was gesturing behind him at a kitchen. I remembered him saying he was spending the day painting at his parent's house, and I inspected the viewable handiwork. He had emerald green and white paint speckled over his cheeks and his backwards baseball hat, and the cabinets behind him were the same green.

I said "Looks good!" in response and sent a cute selfie back of me in my kitchen, still in my blazer and skirt. Though now, my hair had been pulled back into a windblown ponytail since the drive home.

"Ooo Ms. Business, I want to hear all about your meeting," he replied.

I smiled and headed to my room to get changed into more comfortable clothes and then to the bathroom to wash off my make-up. Once I was set up in the living room with my take-out and a seltzer, I replied with a rundown of the meeting. We chatted back and forth about the meeting, his painting, and about the books we were reading. He was reading the book I had given him and liked it so far. Our texting was flirtatious but tame compared to our time in the office last night. When we said goodnight, I was tempted to have him come over to spend the night with me, but I was nervous about taking the lead. Maybe what we shared in the office was a fluke? Maybe he was just feeling horny, and I was the nearest female? No, I had more faith in his control than that. There was likely an explanation for what happened, and it probably wasn't that he was actually interested in me. He was incredibly attractive, outgoing, and had women panting over him in the store every day. I was... a bookworm. I was plain looking, introverted, and very much so did not have men panting over me in the grocery store. It had to be a fluke. An accident. A silly little fling to make his job more interesting.

I spent a long time reading before letting myself go to sleep, knowing I had to work overnight tomorrow. I was reading a fantasy story, and it helped distract me from my worries about Benjamin. Despite being exhausted, it took no effort to stay awake reading. Staying awake to read had never been my problem. In fact, I finished the book I was reading and checked the library's online catalog for the second in the series before even looking at the clock. It was well after two in the morning, so I located the book on the library's website and promptly collapsed into bed.

Tuesday was a slow start. I listened to an audiobook while I worked on planning my café menu. The windows in my kitchen were open and a cool fall breeze blew in. It was perfect weather for a hot cup of coffee and a good book. The second book of the fantasy series I had read the night before was still on my mind with the biggest book hangover. I needed to go to the library before work.

I got dressed for my shift in a pair of jeans and a cream knit sweater. I wore a matching bra and panty set just in case. If Benjamin could use me as a fun fling to make the workday go faster, then I could do the same to him. Even if he wasn't interested in a relationship with me, I could still have fun. The bra and panties were light pink with little white lace trim. It was a soft ribbed cotton set, and I hadn't worn it yet. I had been saving it for a special occasion. And I hoped the end of our shift would be that special occasion. I cleaned up my apartment and changed the sheets on my bed in case we came back here. I left my apartment with a smile on my face and breath mints in my purse.

As I drove past Oscar's to get to the library, I saw that the Schmidt's furniture store had a For Sale sign on the front window. A few men were loading a truck with their remaining stock and the elderly couple was helping as much as they could from their hunched over places on the sidewalk. The Schmidt's furniture store had been there for decades and had been almost always closed lately. There was always a sign detailing when they'd be back from visiting this grandchild or that one. They were kind people, but I hadn't seen them in a while.

That store would be the absolute best location for my bookstore and café. It was in the cute and historic part of town and the inside still had the original red brick walls and wood flooring. I had been in the store many times before, so I knew the inside well. I could see rows and rows of bookshelves, tables and chairs for the café, a long pastry cabinet, and maybe even a stage for readings. The front of the store had sunny windows, and I could arrange comfy chairs and plants there. My heart was racing with all the possibilities. It was a larger space than I had thought I would want, but I knew as soon as I saw the For Sale sign that I needed it. This was it! This was the space I had been searching for!

I pulled into the library's parking lot and parked sloppily near the back. I called the bank and set up a meeting for tomorrow morning at eight when Donnie, the loan officer, got in. The design manuals from the business furniture store were still in my purse, and I pulled them out to study them again. I wanted the dark brown metal shelving, the tan leather armchairs, the wooden plant stands, the gold lamps for accent coloring, and the dark wood tables. I rummaged in my car for a pen and made little stars next to the furniture I wanted. The designer didn't need to pick everything out for me. I was building this store on my own and I wasn't about to outsource the work. I pulled up my phone where I had a document outlining what I estimated to be my expenses in the first year of operation. It was a project from one class I had taken in business school and I had worked diligently on it. I wanted to have a solid number when I walked into the bank tomorrow morning. Being prepared and informed would look good to the loan officer.

Eventually, I ran into the library and found the book I wanted. My delay in the parking lot caused me to be a few minutes late to work, but within the twelve-minute rule. Not that Oscar would make me leave on an overnight shift. I could have been an hour late and he would still be happy to see me arrive.

It turned out that he didn't even notice my tardiness. The

store was packed full of people who had nothing to do other than go grocery shopping at nine at night on a Tuesday. It had been happening more and more frequently now that the local schools were back in session. We saw parents coming in after work, extra-curricular activities, and after the kids had gone to bed to do their grocery shopping. In previous years, Oscar had a "soft close" where the store technically had closed at nine at night, but he allowed people in for another hour to chase those later sales. Now that we were open all night, it was just a busy start to the overnight shift. We kept the music calming and the store announcements to a minimum to create a less stressful environment and someone was dedicated to restocking the essentials like milk, eggs, bread, breakfast cereal, and diapers. Oscar had a finger on the pulse of his clientele, and I respected his awareness. It wasn't something I saw in bigger stores and was something that drove me to want to open my business.

Oscar was working a register, a rare sight as he had number dyslexia that caused him to have to concentrate harder on the numbers when counting and giving change. He was always nervous about getting the change wrong and making people mad, but nobody was ever mad at Oscar. I approached him and he jumped up to let me take over the register. Benjamin was at the register next to mine and he spun on his stool to wink at me in greeting. James was impatiently waving Oscar down from where he was stocking bread. Oscar's mustache was bristling as he stomped over to the teenager, who was eager to leave.

Our shift was busy with customers until about midnight, when it was like a ghost town. I had been left with the task to deep clean the cold produce shelving. I was wrist deep in decayed lettuce, listening to my audiobook, when I heard the crackle of the store's speaker system. "Layla, please report to aisle five. Layla, to aisle five."

I stopped and looked around to see Benjamin hanging up the phone next to the furthest register before disappearing into the aisle. I had been so involved in my task and audiobook that I hadn't been paying attention to what he was doing. Did he have a cleaning task in the baking aisle? Or was it inventory? I took off my gloves that I had worn to clean in and set my phone and ear buds on the cleaning cart. Aisle five was baking ingredients and spices. Was there a flour spill?

It was just as my back slammed into the shelving and the back of my head knocked over a row of decorative sprinkles that I remembered that this was the one aisle in the entire store that the security cameras did not reach. People could be seen entering and exiting the aisle, but not what they did in said aisle. Oscar had fretted about the blind spot when the cameras were installed earlier in the year, but as Benjamin's hands gripped my hips and his lips crashed into mine, I was grateful for the security blind spot.

13

I gasped in shock and then giggled when I realized what was happening.

"Sorry if I scared you," he chuckled against my lips.

"It's okay, it's a welcome shock," I said and rolled my hips against his.

He groaned and gripped both of my hands in one of his and lifted them above my head to pin against the shelf above me. My legs were around his hips as he held me up. His lips reclaimed mine in a hot, wet kiss. His breath fanned over my face after taking a shaking inhale. He was desperate for this. For me. I wanted to claw through his clothes, but he was holding both of my wrists in one of his strong hands. I settled for rolling my hips against his in a rhythm to suggest how I would ride him if he'd let me. He groaned against my lips as he pressed into me even harder. I could feel the solid pressure of his erection in his jeans straining against his fly.

"I've been waiting for this," he said in a panting whisper. The rough scrape of my panties and jeans against my skin made my pussy feel hot and oversensitive as I sought the right angle to grind on him.

"Waiting to get interrupted by a customer again?" I giggled breathlessly. I had been hoping to take Benjamin back to my apartment after work or be taken back to his. But I would certainly accept being ravaged in the baking aisle as long as we weren't interrupted.

"I locked the doors," he said and kissed down my neck. I moaned at the prospect of being undisturbed and the sucking kiss he was giving my collar bone. Encouraged by my moan, he slid his hand down to grasp my breast through my shirt and bra. His large grip encompassed the entire breast and squeezed. I strained my hands in his grasp. I wanted to touch him. To feel his body.

Our uneven rutting against each other had me sliding down until I was almost standing. He let my arms go after I tugged deliberately on them. Standing on my tiptoes, I was face to face with him as he stooped to kiss me. I gripped the back of his neck and held him to me as we kissed, hot and slow. He slid a foot between my shoes and knocked my legs apart and bent forward to continue the kiss. One hand held me around my back to my hip and the other slid three fingers over my jean covered pussy. I gasped at the sensation. After the grinding against denim and ribbed cotton panties, the touch of his fingers over the same materials felt intensified. I felt liquid pool at my entrance, and I was sure I'd soak through. He slid three fingers, one on either side of my mound and one in the center on the seam of my jeans, up and down and I could have come apart right there.

"Oh, yeah?" he asked with a small chuckle.

"Yeah," I sighed and curled my fingers into his hair.

"It's that easy to make you come on my fingers?" he said against my lips.

"Yeah," I repeated, not able to formulate a more eloquent response than that.

He hummed his approval. "That's a good girl," he said huskily.

I would have come right then and there if he hadn't removed his hand from my pussy to open my jeans. I whimpered at the lack of contact and the promise of more as he let go of me entirely to rip my jeans down my legs. The wetness of my panties caused them to stick to my jeans, and they remained on my thighs when the materials disconnected at my knees. Benjamin kissed my thighs right above my panties and I realized he was on his knees.

"These are cute," he said and licked the inside of my thigh.

"My bra matches," I told him with a breathless giggle.

"Oh, were you planning on this happening?" he teased as he tore them down my legs to tangle with my jeans around my feet.

"Hoping," I said as he looked up at me, sitting back on his knees, his hands on my thighs.

"In the office or an aisle?" he asked, his eyes glinting in the fluorescent lights.

"In my bed," I clarified. "Or yours."

"See, I was hoping it would start right here," he said in a quiet murmur just as he licked a languid line up the slit of my pussy.

My breath caught in my throat and my eyes rolled back as he licked slow and long like we had all night. The sudden pleasure was so intense that I could not even moan. I didn't even breathe. The grinding against denim, the light touch through two layers, and now his mouth on me. He had barely touched me and I was near coming. I wanted more. I tried to spread my legs further. My sneaker squeaked on the waxed linoleum before stopping where my jeans stretched. I groaned in frustration and Benjamin puffed a laugh across my over sensitive and needy pussy. He ripped one shoe off my foot and shoved my jeans and panties over the freed ankle before slinging that leg over his shoulder.

"Come here, I need a taste of you," he growled deep in his throat. "Fucking soaked. Beautiful."

I cried out as his tongue lapped at my entrance. I used one hand to brace myself on the shelving behind me and one hand gripped his curled hair. My legs were trembling with pleasure and anticipation. I wanted to curl my leg around his neck and pull him into me further, but I refrained from putting him in a headlock. Instead, I let out a whining demand for more and was satisfied when one hand joined his mouth. He slid two fingers through my arousal before slowly pushing into me. The butterflies and clenching muscles that had started the kiss yesterday were in full force now and I felt my pussy clenching almost rhythmically around his fingers.

"I knew I would feel it from the inside," he said, his breath hot against my skin. "Those greedy pussy pulsations."

I was about to retort that it only made sense that if he could feel it outside, then he could feel it inside, when he curled those fingers and worked his wrist. My breathing had been irregular and gasping before but was now ragged and desperate with intermittent whimpers. My legs shook violently, and I gripped his hair tight in my fist as he curled his fingers towards the front of my body over and over and sucked loudly and sloppily. Benjamin gave a "Ha!" of exaltation when he realized he was making me come in rivers down my thighs. He adjusted his position to get a stronger angle and continued his work, tapping at the sensitive spot inside me that had me seeing stars while working his wrist back and forth, adding pressure on my entrance.

"That's a good girl," he said between loud sucks. "Keep coming for me. Let's see how much you got."

My entire body felt feverish with pleasure and shame, and I was sure I was about to pass out. I closed my eyes and held on with both hands on the shelving. It felt like every bit of liquid had just drained out of my body and I was still just on the cusp of an orgasm. I let out a hoarse cry as it finally broke over me like a shock wave. I rode his fingers and his face through it. He moaned against my pussy as he sucked and licked.

When I came back into my body, I looked down to see him grinning up at me. His chin and front of his shirt were wet, and he wiped his mouth with the back of his hand.

"Oh," I said, embarrassed and looking him over. "I'm sor-"

"Don't you dare apologize," he said with a shake of his head. "I fucking love it."

"Oh," I said again, but with hesitant acceptance now. "I kind of forgot I did that."

He snorted a laugh as he stood. "Well, I never will."

I looked at the bulge in his jeans as the hunger for him resurfaced.

"It must have been a long time if you forgot," he said and stood next to me, leaning against the shelves.

I considered. "It's been... maybe a few years. But I've never... with a guy."

"You've never had an orgasm with a man?" he asked incredulously.

"No, I mean, I have. But not like..." I blushed and gestured at the wet front of his shirt.

"Is this a special occasion thing?" he asked with a mischievous glint in his eyes. I nodded. "Am I the first person you've squirted on?"

I nodded again, my blush even deeper now. I felt sweaty but still needy. It was his turn to come undone now, and I would have time to feel embarrassed and shameful later.

He groaned and chuckled. "I fucking love it. And here we are in fucking aisle five at work. I'm so turned on it's ridiculous."

I shook my head with a smile on my lips. I dropped to my knees in front of him and immediately began undoing his thick leather belt and jeans. He took a shuddering breath and lifted the hem of his t-shirt over his abs. He stroked my hair back from my face and looked down at me with dark eyes and a smirk. I could smell the clean scent of his laundry detergent and the pheromones men gave off. It wasn't exactly a scent but an animal understanding, and I certainly understood that I wanted Benjamin. I opened his jeans and pulled them down to his muscular and tattooed thighs. He was huge and hard in his black boxer briefs. They were soft and worn, like they were his favorite pair, with Calvin Klein printed along the waistband. I licked a stripe along where the waistband gave way to skin on his lower abs. He had a slight Adonis belt, and I laved my tongue in the indents on both sides.

His breath hitched as I slid my fingertips in the waistband of his boxer briefs and tugged them down. His cock sprung free and bobbed almost comically for a second before I dove forward. I was still sliding his boxer briefs down his thighs to his jeans when I wrapped my mouth around him. He hissed out a long "fuck," and gripped my hair at the back of my head. I smiled around him before pulling off of him. The corners of my mouth had caught on his skin, so I looked up at him and licked around my lips. My mouth was watering at the prospect of his cock in my mouth, so it only took a second of looking up at him, with his chest heaving and mouth open, to gather enough saliva. I lowered my mouth down on to him slowly with a slight suck, still looking up at him. His eyes were intense on my mouth until I had taken him all the way in, and my lips touched the base. Coarse hair at the base tickled my lips, and I wiggled them around his cock. His eyes closed and his jaw relaxed in a sighing moan. His grip on my hair tugged me back. I had just been about to pull back since his cock blocked where my nasal airway connected to my throat, and I wasn't able to breathe around him all the way in. We both heaved for air. He leaned his head back against the shelf, knocking over a few cans of frosting. They rolled to the ground next to me, the lids popping off and exposing the silver foil safety seal.

I pulled off of him with a *pop* and licked up and down his shaft with a swirl at his head. He moaned and his belly heaved as he panted. I reached a hand up to cup his balls gently and he swore.

"Fuck, Layla," he groaned out, his grip on my hair so tight it brought tears to my eyes. But I didn't stop. I wanted to see him lose it. I wanted to see him come. Giving his balls a light squeeze, I bobbed up and down on him and swirled my tongue.

He moaned deep and long as my nose touched his lower abs as I took him as deep as I could, fighting the involuntary gag.

"Good girl, just hold it there. Holy shit. So good. You feel amazing. Keep going," he stuttered out in a deep voice. I had always been good at following directions. I stopped bobbing on his cock and let him rest in my mouth and throat. I gagged a few times around him at the weight resting on my tongue but refrained from pulling all the way off of him. "Good fucking girl. Your mouth is so fucking hot I want to- fuck, Layla. I'm going to come."

I hummed hungrily around him. The vibrations must have added another level of sensation because he came with a shout. The salty taste of him filled my mouth in spurts as he came. He curled down towards me, both hands on the back of my head, as his inked thighs trembled on either side of me. I swallowed him down with a bit of difficulty, seeing as he was still taking up much of the room in my mouth. I sat back on my heels and looked up at him as he stroked my hair. He smiled at me with hooded, satiated eyes when he saw me looking. He yanked his pants up over his ass and tucked his still hard cock into his boxer briefs before sliding to sit on the floor in front of me.

"Wow," he said and leaned forward to kiss me. He was still panting, and I could see the pulse pounding in his tattooed neck. We kissed, tasting ourselves on each other's tongues for a while before our heart rates returned to normal.

I leaned against his chest as he stroked my hair and neck softly, raising goosebumps and making me sleepy. "I could go to sleep here," I said with a yawn.

"I'm over this overnight shift thing," Benjamin said with a

sigh. "It's been fucking with my sleep so much that I can almost never sleep when I need to."

"Same. Right before the festival, I felt like I was near a mental breaking point. I've been thinking about asking Oscar to take me off nights," I said, and my eyes fluttered as he stroked lightly around my ear.

"Why didn't you?" he asked. "You were a total brat that week. I figured you just needed to get laid."

I snorted. "You. I didn't want to stop working with you."

He chuckled, the sound reverberating in his chest under my ear. "I didn't ask him to stop because of you, too."

I lifted my head to look into his warm brown eyes. "We were out here suffering through sleep deprivation when we could have been sleeping and having orgasms?"

He laughed, tipping his head back, and it was his genuine laugh. "I guess so."

We got dressed and cleaned up the various messes we'd made in the baking aisle. We stopped occasionally for a kiss, but we cleaned up and dressed in time to finish the tasks we'd been assigned for the night. When the morning crew arrived, we were presentable and acting normal until Benjamin pressed me against my car in the parking lot.

"Come home with me," he whispered against my neck.

I opened my mouth to agree when I remembered my meeting with the bank in a few hours. I sighed. "I can't, I have a meeting at eight."

"Skip it," he said with a nibble to my neck.

I squeaked and shook him off with a giggle. "I can't. It's super important and with the bank. I need to make a good impression."

He nodded in understanding. I wanted to tell him about the space next to Oscar's store, but I didn't want to jinx my luck. I kissed him slowly and softly before pulling away.

"Alright," he exhaled. "Go be a badass business woman. I won't be able to see you until our shift on Thursday morning. I'm finishing up with my parents in their kitchen this afternoon and then it's my nephew's birthday at the arcade."

"Can I come over after the party?" I asked and traced my fingers over the now dry t-shirt on his chest. I bit my lip and looked up at him through my lashes.

He smirked and kissed my nose. "I want time with you. I want to wine and dine you first. As much as I want to pound you into my mattress, I want to… romance you first."

I giggled. "We've had a date already, though."

"I remember. But I was on my best behavior, then. I was doing my best not to scare you off," he said and tucked my hair behind my ear.

"That's why you didn't hold my hand," I pouted.

He smirked again. "I was afraid that if I touched you, I'd lose my control."

"Just holding my hand would do that?" I asked and cocked my head to the side.

"I didn't think I'd be able to stop at just holding your fucking hand, Layla," he said with mock irritation. "Remember watching the sunset?" I nodded. "If there wasn't a family with children and other people every five feet, I would have thrown you down into the sand and had you coming all over my cock right then and there. But we still had to go to work that night and I knew that there would be no way I'd keep my hands off of you once I'd gotten started."

I was blushing now and bit my lip again. He thumbed it away from my teeth.

"Does that answer your question?"

I nodded.

"Is it alright if we wait until after our Thursday shift for me to make you dinner before I fuck you into next year?" he asked.

I nodded again and gulped.

"Good girl," he said with a sly smile before stepping back. "See you tomorrow, little one."

He got into his car and drove off with a wink while I fumbled to get into my car and start the ignition. In the silence of my car, I had a moment of clarity. Holy shit, I had just had sex with Benjamin. Well, oral sex. In aisle five at Oscar's store. I blushed, remembering how I had behaved. I had been wanton. Shameless. All I could do now was laugh alone in my car. He truly liked me. I don't think a guy who didn't like me would have continued to wear a t-shirt that I had soaked for the rest of the shift. I think he dried it with a hand dryer in the bathroom, but still. He wore it. I felt a little embarrassed that I had come so hard our first time together, but also selfishly satiated. I was excited for Thursday night, that's for sure. If oral and his hands had done that, I couldn't imagine what would come next.

14

At home, I took a nice hour-long nap, a shower, and got ready for my meeting at the bank. I dressed in black dress pants, a pink lace blouse, black heels, and held a folder of my accumulated plans for my bookstore. My hair was in a sleek ponytail, and I wore make-up to look and feel more confident. I arrived at the bank five minutes early and I waited in the lobby, trying not to look nervous.

Donnie came out of his office at eight on the nose. He was wearing worn khakis and a polo with the bank's logo on it. "Miss Avery?"

I turned to him swiftly. "That's me, hello." I reached out a hand to shake. He looked startled at my hand, like he rarely shook hands with customers. I instantly felt silly. He shook my hand, his grip soft and limp wristed. Gross.

"Come into my office," he said in a dismissive tone. Like I was inconveniencing his day by having him do his job.

He sat in a creaking leather chair behind his desk, and I perched on the end of the stiff armchair in front of him. I sat up straight and crossed my ankles, my hands folded on my folder on my lap. Donnie looked almost exactly as I'd known him in school. He was a few years above me and was a star player on the football team. He had gone off to play for college and came back here a few years later. I didn't keep up with many of my high school classmates, but I knew who ended up returning to our small town when they came into Oscar's doing their shopping.

"I hear you're in to see about a loan?" Donnie, *the loan officer*, said. His blue eyes were just as piercing as they were in school. His blonde hair was thinner and lighter than a decade ago, but he looked very much the same.

"Yes, I am hoping to purchase the property on Old Main Street where the furniture store was," I explained.

"Oh yeah? What for?" he looked me over head to toe.

I remained sitting upright confidently. "I want to open a bookstore and café."

"A bookstore?" he wrinkled his nose. "Do that many people still read?"

I had come prepared with statistics about the increase of book sales, especially indie books, in the last few years, so I opened my folder and presented him with the data. I spoke in a calm, informative, and slow voice. When he tilted his head as he listened, I partially mirrored him.

"Do you have a financial plan?" He asked, satisfied with the statistics.

"Yes, in fact, I do," I said and slid my current bank statement with my savings and the rest of my financial plan for the store across his glass top desk.

Donnie raised an eyebrow before picking it up, and I gave a polite smile.

He checked the time on his computer; I looked at my watch. He shuffled his feet under the desk; I smoothed a hand over my pants.

"You're going to make coffee at this store?" he asked in a tone that didn't sound like asking. The lack of rising intonation on the question let me know he wasn't taking me seriously.

"Correct," I said, treating his question as a statement. "I will also have tea and some bakery items."

"It'll be a girly space, yeah?" He almost scoffed.

"I believe a bookstore and café to be gender neutral," I said with a small shake of my head.

"Sure," he said and waved it off. "Why do you believe you need that big of a space?"

"I believe having ample space to browse, read, and relax will greatly increase a person's interest in buying a book. If they feel relaxed and comfortable, they will shop longer. My store will be a place that customers return to often not only for the books and coffee, but for the atmosphere and events," I explained in my best business woman voice.

"Events?" he asked dubiously.

"Yes. Book clubs, signings, theme parties, game nights, craft nights, and movie events. To name a few," I said and smiled.

He gave a disinterested smile in return to be polite. He looked over the rest of the paperwork I had and then sighed. "Alright, I'll run some numbers. It's all up to your credit, now."

"Thank you for your time," I smiled, trying not to show my elation. Successful business men *expect* things to go their way. They don't gush with gratitude when they win.

Donnie typed away at his computer for a few minutes, and I

remained poised in my seat. I answered banking questions as he asked them and didn't rush to get all the paperwork I had prepared off of his desk. Those were his copies, and if he didn't need them, he could throw them away later. I was not to scramble around apologetically.

A few quiet minutes later, he sat back in his chair, looking at his computer. "Well, Miss Avery- Layla. Did we go to school together?"

"I believe you were a few years ahead of me," I said.

He looked at me with squinted eyes, like he was trying to remember me looking younger. "Were you a cheerleader?"

"No," I said without distaste.

"Dance team?"

"No."

"Marching band?"

"No. Debate and drama," I replied, taking him out of his misery.

"Hm," he hummed derisively. "We weren't in the same circles then."

"No, I guess not."

"I miss those days, don't you?" He said wistfully.

"Not in the slightest," I said politely.

He looked confused but then looked back at his computer. "Well, Layla. You've been pre-approved for a loan for the store. It looks like if you buy the store front you were looking at, you'll be tight on funds to decorate all girly and such."

I shook off his comment. "Thank you, I'm thrilled we could arrange this."

He printed off my approval letter and signed it. He jumped

out of his seat to shake my hand after I stood and reached out. After making a man jump out of his seat to shake my hand, I smiled wider and more triumphantly. I left with my shoulders back and head high. I left the papers from my speech scattered on his desk for him to clean up.

Upon leaving, I contacted a commercial realtor. I had saved her business card for months, knowing that I wanted to work with her when it came time to buy the store's property. It just so happened that she was the selling agent. She was in the area and available, so we met at her office to get started.

Susan was the mom of a flock of siblings that went to school with me. She was always involved in the school events, and she got her real estate license once all of her kids were in school. Her children were involved in many activities, dressed well, and respectful. So, I trusted her to get shit done.

As I was parking at Susan's office, my phone chimed. I looked to see a message from Benjamin. I smiled widely as I opened and read it. "Just woke up from the craziest dream that we hooked up last night in the baking aisle. Tell me that actually happened."

"I had sprinkles in my hair this morning," I texted back and sent him a cute selfie of me in my business attire.

Almost immediately, he sent me a picture of him in bed. He was at least shirtless, the sheets low on his hips, showing off the expanse of muscle and ink. His hair was messy, and his face was relaxed in a lazy smile that caused a heat to settle low in my belly. Then I remembered our conversation from months ago about him sleeping naked. "Wish I was there," I said to him. "Headed into a meeting."

"That's my girl," he replied. "Go and kick some ass!"

I was grinning ear to ear as I entered Susan's office. Susan was quick and efficient at her job- like I knew she would be. She had all of my paperwork organized and ready to be filled out when I walked in and I had an offer in for the property in less than an hour.

I was exhausted when I got home early in the afternoon, but I had planning to do. I made myself a latte and sat at my kitchen table to make plans. Susan had given me the layout and measurements of the furniture store and I chose the furniture I wanted from the catalogs I had been holding on to. There were a few walls that needed to be painted, but most of the property had original red brick walls and amazing wooden flooring. I knew I wanted better lighting and chose some beautiful gold chandeliers. I spent hours at the table working and planning. It was truly coming together.

Benjamin and I traded flirty texts when he was able, but no more pictures until his nephew's party. It was near midnight when my phone chimed with a picture message. I was curled up in bed reading the second book in the fantasy series I was hooked on when I got the message. It was Benjamin, lounging on the bench in the gazebo in town with a mischievous smile.

"Give me ten," was my quickly typed response. A huge grin was plastered to my face as I switched out my worn t-shirt for a short, black nightdress and blew out my candles. The nightdress was a satin material that clung to my skin like a bodycon dress. I typically wore it only when laundry desperately needed done. I applied a light coat of lip balm and brushed my teeth. As an afterthought, I slipped my panties off by the door before putting on my coat. I grabbed my keys and rushed out to my car, hoping

Benjamin had seen my text before he left the gazebo. I realized he might not have been actually inviting me, but I was about to show up, anyway.

15

His car was parked outside the gazebo, and butterflies of excitement erupted in my stomach. I parked next to him and left my keys on the seat. He stood up and watched me get out of my car with a sideways grin. "Hey, little one," he greeted me as I ascended the steps.

"Hey," I said with what I hoped to be a seductive smile. The heat of my breath puffed in front of my face in the cold air. "How was the party?"

"Insane. It was fifteen preschoolers playing arcade games," he chuckled and opened his arms as I approached him.

"I bet you fit right in," I said and let him envelop me in his arms.

"I did, actually," I felt him smile against my skin as he kissed my neck.

I sighed at the contact and slid my hands around to the back of his neck and head.

"I missed you," I said breathlessly as he nipped at my collarbone. A puff of his breath swirled visibly around us as he kissed and sucked at my neck.

"Oh, little one, all I wanted was to see you," he said with a rough voice.

"You see me all the time," I giggled.

"Sure, but now I've tasted you. Now I know what you sound like when you come. What you look like. And, honestly, I'm already addicted," he said. His lips met mine in a scorching kiss.

His hands roamed over my back before sliding under my puffy coat. He pulled at my lips with his in a demanding kiss and I complied happily. Benjamin gripped my ass with both hands hard enough it hurt, but not enough for me to tell him to stop. He kneaded my ass and bunched up my nightgown. My thighs were already slippery with need for him, and I trembled with anticipation. His hard length pressed against my stomach and my mouth watered, remembering the taste of him. When the tips of his fingers grazed over my pussy, we both gasped.

"No panties, huh?" he chuckled. "I guess you understood that this was a booty call."

"Duh," I said and undid the fly on his jeans.

"To be clear," he said and stopped touching me to grab my wrists in his hands. I looked up at him. "To be clear, I want nothing more than to sink my cock into you, but I'm not going to tonight."

"Right, something about wining and dining before sixty-nine-ing," I said dismissively. I didn't need a speech; I just needed his hands and his mouth on me.

He grinned. His white teeth almost shone in the dim fairy lights around the gazebo. He looked seductively menacing. I had been confident and lustful before and now I was a little frightened but a lot desperate for him. I bit my lip and looked up at him through my lashes. His grin turned even more menacing. Like he was going to devour me. An icy wind circled us, and I shivered. My rapid breathing was audible in the town's silence and visible with the cold air. He licked his lips and then bit down on his bottom one with a canine tooth. Now I shivered with adrenaline.

"Right," he finally replied in a deep, almost hoarse voice. "So, here's what's going to happen. We're going to re-do that time when you brought me coffee here in the middle of the night. But this time, when Officer Dan pulls up, it'll be because of a noise complaint. You understand?"

I nodded and swallowed hard.

"Good girl," he said and forcefully moved my hands to be behind my back and gripped in one of his large hands.

Despite his menacing expression made more intimidating with his tattoos and dark clothing, I knew I was safe with him. I knew without a doubt that Benjamin, with his apparent intensities, would never intentionally hurt me. And with that realization, I let my muscles relax into his hold. My coat slid down my shoulder, exposing bare skin to the air. Cold and Benjamin both bit at my skin and I sighed and turned my face into his hair. I kissed his hair just above his ear, as it was all I could reach of him.

He wrapped the arm not holding my hands around me and picked me up. He spun me so my back was against a pillar of the gazebo and set me down. As he kissed me, he pressed his body against mine. I turned my head to gasp for air and he chuckled darkly and kissed a trail down my neck. He didn't stop there and kissed over my satin night dress as he got on his knees before me. He let go of my hands, but my weight leaning back kept them pinned behind me. Benjamin crouched before me for a moment before swearing under his breath and standing back up. He stepped away and emptied his front pockets before kneeling before me again. I looked at the items on the bench: his phone, keys, wallet, a toy car, and a switchblade.

"Odd set of items to carry to a booty call," I whispered.

He looked back at the items and snorted a laugh. "What, you mean you don't always carry a Hotwheels car and a knife? Lame."

"I get the toy car; you were at a kid's party. But a knife?" I asked with a giggle.

"Um, excuse me, I was the hero when I was the only one with a way to cut those dumb zip ties off the new toys," he laughed but was still pushing my nightdress up and over my hips.

He licked a hot line over my pussy, and I whimpered.

"Oh, I thought it was because of your knife play kink," I said breathlessly through a smile.

He stopped licking me to look at the knife, at me, and then back to the knife. His eyebrows were up in interest and his mouth pulled down in a considering frown. He seemed to decide and shook his head and looked back up at me. "Nah, you wouldn't li-"

"Maybe I would," I interrupted him.

He stopped and let out a low moan, resting his forehead against my hip.

"Maybe I would," I repeated myself.

I heard him take a long breath before slowly standing up. He stood so close his clothes brushed against my bare, chilled skin. His exhale was slow and long and puffed over my upturned face.

His eyes were dark and menacing again. He clenched his jaw, and I watched the muscles bunch. He seemed to stand up taller and straighter and he cocked his head to the side, considering me like I was prey. It was like he had just become someone else with that long breath. When he had looked his fill, the corner of one side of his mouth lifted and he turned to his knife. He picked it up and flicked it open. The metal glinted in the moonlight and fairy lights around us. I swallowed and my heart was pounding in my chest. That animal fear upon seeing a weapon meant for me tickled in my spine, swirling and merging with my lust.

This was unlike any experience I had ever had. Nobody had never even tied me up in bed and here I was, jumping headfirst into knife play. I felt like people tended to work their way up to this kink. I was probably going to hate it. But I could always tell him to stop. I relaxed a little knowing I could stop at any time. My hands gripped the cold wood of the gazebo railing on either side of my waist.

He inspected the blade for a second before locking eyes with me and licking along the flat side. I clenched my thighs together, remembering how his tongue felt between them.

"Are you sure, little one?" he asked, a flicker of concern danced over his eyes.

"Oh, yes," I said more bravely than I was feeling.

He smirked and approached me with a deliberate and confident stride. "I can see your pulse," he remarked and pressed the blunt side of the knife against the skin of my neck. My eyes fluttered and closed out of reflex. "Look at me," he demanded quietly.

I looked up at him and he smiled wolfishly. He maintained

eye contact with me as he slid the knife down my neck to my chest. He held the tip against the skin over my heart. "I think-" he started and then swallowed and looked at what he was doing. "I think that this-" quicker than I could have imagined, he flicked an X into my skin. Blood welled up in the thin, shallow lines. "-is going to be mine."

My body shook with adrenaline and cold and a little fear. "It's been. For a while," I whispered, my jaw trembling with my body.

His eyes flicked up to mine with his head still tipped down towards my chest. His pupils dilated. He dipped down slowly, maintaining eye contact, to lick a flat, soft tongue over the cut. I hissed at the sting of contact against the wound. When he pulled back, I saw my blood on his tongue and my head rushed. Two animal instincts warred within me. One was to run. This man in front of me was a predator who would feast on me until I was bones. And the other instinct was to wrap my legs around him and let him sink into me bare. And I realized that was where the beauty and tragedy of femininity rested. A woman's most dangerous natural predator was a man.

Benjamin sank to his knees before me again, this time with the knife against the inside of my thigh. My breath hitched in my throat as he pushed my nightdress back over my hips. He licked over my pussy again and nudged my knees apart. He removed the knife so I could widen my stance and not get cut. Only using the fingertips of the hand not holding the knife, he teased at my wetness before licking it off his fingertips like sugar. Benjamin groaned against me, and the knife returned to my thigh. He removed his fingertips to devour me. He alternated between long licks over my folds and sharp sucks at my clit. Benjamin worked me until I was just at the top of an orgasm when he pulled away from sucking on my clit to gently flick his tongue over it while he looked down and sliced a thin, shallow cut into the inside of my thigh. I had been holding my breath as I was just about to come, and it left me in a sharp exhale. The bite of pain on my thigh was much more than the tiny pricks on my chest. Not so much that I wanted to stop, but more than I had expected. Benjamin let the few beads of blood well up and drip down my leg before he licked along the cut. The pain subsided after the initial sting, and my arousal took over. My head spun. Not from blood loss, there wasn't nearly enough for that. But I felt faint as my body fought to keep up with lust and the feeling of going against my bodily instincts to run.

"Please," I begged him like I had in the office that day of our first kiss. My voice was strained and breathless as I whined.

He grinned up at me with my blood on his lips. "Did you want to come?"

"Yes! Yes, please," I pleaded. My body felt so overheated that I wasn't cold in the chilly fall night air. Every pant and word from our mouths left steam billowing into the air, but I was warm.

Maintaining eye contact he sucked at my clit again until my head tipped back at the wave of incoming pleasure. But he pulled away again, my core painfully clenching as the stimulation ceased. He sliced a line into my unmarred thigh. He licked up the blood the same as on the other thigh. This time I was whimpering and keening helplessly as my legs trembled. I begged him over and over to let me come. My voice sounded unfamiliar to me at that moment. He huffed a laugh over my skin and returned to licking and sucking on my pussy. This time, when I was just about to come, I bit my lip and kept as quiet as possible so that he would let me ride it through. But he sat back on his heels and grinned roguishly up at me. A deep, desperate groan escaped me, and I snaked a hand between my legs.

"No way," he scolded and pulled my hand away. "I want us to come together, so you have to wait."

He finished undoing the fly on his jeans that I had started earlier, and shoved his jeans and boxer briefs down over his ass. His cock sprung free, and I dropped to my knees in front of where he was still kneeling. I bent forward and took him into my mouth. My pussy was still painfully clenching around nothing as I sucked him into my mouth over and over. Benjamin groaned and fisted my hair at the back of my head. He had dropped the knife on the ground next to us and was now forcefully guiding my head by my hair. He mumbled praises as I choked and gagged. When he was all the way in my throat, his thick cock blocked my airway, so I was heaving for breath and gagging every time he pulled my head back. My eyes were streaming, and I was shifting my hips trying for different friction against my pussy.

"Come up here," he moaned out. I sat up and he adjusted so that I could straddle his legs. "Fuck, the ground is cold," he hissed out as his bare ass came in contact with the concrete. It was then that I came back to reality enough to remember we were in the gazebo in the center of town. There were pumpkins and bales of hay around us with little fairy lights. Tomorrow families would be here taking pictures for their Christmas cards and people would walk their dogs before work. I would have giggled at how naughty we were being if I wasn't so absolutely desperate to come and for him to come with me. I quickly straddled his thighs and wrapped a hand around his cock. "No, touch yourself, I want to see it," he panted as he lifted his sweater over his stomach. "I want to see how you make yourself come."

My hand dove greedily to my pussy and started rubbing circles around my clit. He gripped his cock in his fist and stroked in a steady rhythm. We watched each other drive our pleasure higher and higher, our breaths panting and moaning. Watching his hand on his cock, the rippling of his tattooed abs and arms, and hearing him moan my name had me coming in seconds. I gripped his shirt at his chest as I rode my hand through my orgasm. Benjamin watched me, face to face as I came. His jaw dropped open, and he panted as he stared at me. His cheeks were red with a flush of pleasure and he glanced down after I came. Benjamin's eyes trailed the thin line of blood that had dripped down my chest, between my breasts, and disappeared under my nightdress. His eyes strayed further to where blood was smeared on my thighs and over his jeans from the twin cuts. And then they settled on where my arousal left a wet patch on his jeans and the concrete below us.

"Fucking loved your mouth on my cock," he breathed. "Keep touching your pussy." I obeyed. "Mmm, good girl. Let me see you come again. I love to watch you come."

Benjamin let go of his cock to use that hand to gather some of my arousal. My hips jerked at his contact with my pussy. He rubbed until his hand was sufficiently lubricated and he brought it back to his cock.

I kept up rubbing my clit while I reached my other hand behind me to finger my pussy from the back. The back of my hand on my clit kept brushing against his cock and his hand as he stroked himself. When he rested his forehead against my shoulder and shuddered out a desperate moan, I came again. My back arched, and I worked twice as hard to chase my orgasm. Benjamin's free hand gripped my nightgown at the middle of my back and pulled me towards him in time with his hand as if I was riding him. His eyes squinted shut against my shoulder as he let out a guttural moan. His hips rolled and caused his cock to press against my slowing hand. He groaned out a chant, "Fuck, Layla, fuck, Layla," just before his hand stuttered and he pulled me even closer as he came. His abs clenched and released over and over as his fist kept up a tight but slow movement. His throaty moan vibrated against my shoulder and chest as his come coated his fist and our stomachs. He slowed his hand and our combined breathing followed.

I giggled at our predicament now as the chill of the air crept into my awareness. He chuckled, still catching his breath, and wiped his hand off on his jeans. I was still giggling as he leaned back on his hands and looked at me with a lazy smile. "What?"

"I'm never going to walk by here and not think of tonight," I said between giggles. "We're in the town gazebo."

He looked around and said, "Yeah, I know. Pretty hot, huh?"

"Actually, it's freezing," I replied.

He looked down at my goosebump covered thighs. "Yeah, let's get you warmed up in my car."

We hurried down the gazebo steps to his car and got in. He started the engine and the heater.

"I can't believe we did that in the middle of town," I giggled again.

"I can't believe we did that at all," he said and contemplated me.

Feeling self-conscious, I looked down. "Was it too much?"

I knew it was too much. On every level. But after all this time, didn't we deserve "too much?"

"It was amazing. You're fucking perfect," he said and his face relaxed in a smile. "I was just thinking that I had never thought you'd be into anything not...."

"Vanilla," I finished for him. "You thought I'd be vanilla."

He gave a lopsided grin. "Hey, don't knock vanilla. I do love vanilla. But yeah, I guess I didn't think you'd...."

"Be a freak?"

"Sure."

"I didn't know either. Shocking, I know," I said and sighed. "I didn't think I would like the knife and blood. But it was actually pretty hot."

"Speaking of, did I hurt you?" he asked and reached for my thighs.

The cuts had since closed. They had not been deep cuts to begin with. I didn't even feel them now. "No, I'm fine. We're a mess, though."

He snorted a laugh, looking us over.

Lights flashed behind us, and Benjamin looked in the rearview mirror. "It's Officer Dan," he sighed.

"Um, we're both covered in blood and come," I hissed and looked behind us.

"Quick, make out with me," Benjamin said and grabbed my face. His lips were tensely pressed against mine when a knock sounded from his window. He rolled it down, and I worked to cover the blood on my legs with my coat. "Hey Officer Dan," Benjamin said cheerfully.

"Ben, is everything okay? Layla?" he shone his flashlight into the car, and I blocked the bright light.

"Yeah," Benjamin said. "We're good."

"Just meeting to... talk," I said.

Benjamin snorted.

"Alright, you two know that it's after one in the morning?" Officer Dan asked.

"We're night shifters, just like you. This is our afternoon," Benjamin said casually.

"Get off the roads, you two," he said in a tone that said he was dismissing us for now.

Benjamin gave him a salute before he pulled away.

"Ugh, now everyone is going to find out about us," I said tiredly.

"Is that so bad?" Benjamin asked hesitantly.

"No, I just... maybe want it to be only us a little longer," I said. He took my hand and kissed my knuckles.

"It'll always be only us," he breathed. "Whatever the people of our town say has no impact on how I feel."

I considered him for a moment while he looked back at me. His curly blonde hair was getting long, a piece fell in front of his warm brown eyes. His leather jacket was open on his chest and his sweater was stuck to the skin of his stomach after our time in the gazebo. He smelled like sweat, come, Old Spice deodorant, and leather. All it took was a few orgasms to shift my obsession with him to love. I swallowed down that oxytocin and hormone induced thought and looked away.

"We were like two minutes from getting put in jail for indecent exposure," I said, changing the topic.

"Let's... not think about that anymore," Benjamin said, and I laughed.

"Can you imagine Donna hearing about it?"

"Honestly, I think she'd make peanut butter bars in celebration," he chuckled. "She's been trying to get me to ask you out for a few years now."

"Well, why didn't you?" I asked, feeling self-conscious again.

"I thought you weren't interested in me. You would never flirt back," he said with a shrug.

"You flirt with everyone!" I exclaimed, not about to take responsibility.

"Yeah, but you said nothing back, so I thought you were for sure not into me," he said, and leaned his head back against the seat.

I shook my head. "I didn't want you to think I was silly and obsessed with you."

He laughed at my confession.

"I want you to come home with me," I said, feeling emboldened.

"Not tonight. Remember, I want a good date first," he reminded me in a whisper.

"Right, wine and dine and all that," I said and put my coat back on.

"You got it, little one," he said as I leaned forward to kiss him. Our kiss was slow and sweet, and I didn't want to pull away.

"I'll see you in the morning," I breathed.

"See you in a few hours," he amended and kissed me again.

It was after two in the morning when I got home, showered, and fell into bed. A smile was plastered to my face as I set my alarm for tomorrow.

16

I arrived at work exhausted and a few minutes late. Benjamin was still in the staff room when I walked in. He was leaning on the doorway to Oscar's office and talking with our loveable boss. He winked at me as I hurried in the door. I smiled and couldn't help the blush that crept over my cheeks. I clocked in and donned my apron. We had moved on to our deep red aprons for fall after the apple festival, and I found I liked that color best. I tied the thick canvas strings behind my back until warm fingers joined mine and finished tying the knots. A kiss was pressed to the nape of my neck.

"Good morning," I whispered.

"Good morning," Benjamin replied. "I can't wait for our date later."

"Hmm," I hummed. "What are we doing tonight?"

"I'm cooking for you," he said as I turned around to face him.

"What are you making?" I asked, and let my eyes rake over him unapologetically. He was wearing a navy-blue polo, his work khakis, and had cleanly styled hair. It wasn't the leather jacket and jeans I liked best on him, but was how I came to know him first.

"I was thinking of a nice ribeye, a baked potato, and a spinach salad. Red wine to drink. Chocolate strawberries for dessert," he murmured and traced a finger on my polo over where he had carved an X in my chest last night.

"Sounds perfect," I sighed and shivered at his touch.

The staff doors swung open, and Donna came stomping in. "Oscar!" she shouted and marched over to his office.

Benjamin stepped back from me with a smirk. "Oscar actually wants to meet with you. Likely after he's done getting his ass handed to him by whatever is up Donna's."

"No more nights?" I guessed.

Benjamin winked at me with a click of his tongue. He turned and went through the swinging doors. I could hear his call of "Alright, who tormented Donna?" through the gaps in the door.

I cleaned the coffee mugs in the sink and made my cup before Donna left Oscar's office. She seemed in a better mood than entering, so I assumed Oscar would need a cup of coffee as well. I entered the office, fresh mugs in hand, to see a harassed Oscar at his desk. His face lit up when he saw me and even more when he saw I was handing him a drink.

"Oh, Layla, thank you," he said gratefully as he took a sip. "Benjamin told you to come in?"

"Yeah, I just waited until Donna came out," I said and sat in the old pharmacy chair before his desk.

Upon hearing her name, his mustache wilted. He rolled his eyes and moved some papers around on his desk. "Well, her issues are her own. I wanted to call you in and talk to you about something else."

"And here I am," I said, and sipped my coffee.

"I wanted you to know that I am forever thankful for your eager participation in our overnight shift… experiment. I hope you found it helpful in saving for your own store?" Oscar asked, his watery blue eyes on me earnestly.

"It was very helpful, yes. How do you think it's going so far having overnights?" I asked.

He grimaced. I knew it wasn't financially a good plan, but it wasn't my place to say anything. Besides, he was the one who let it go on all summer. "Not as I'd hoped. So, Layla, I have decided to end the overnights. As of today, we will no longer have overnight shifts. Benjamin suggested you and he both spoke of how it was becoming detrimental to your health. And I- I can't have that. You two are like my own children."

"Oh, Oscar," I said, feeling choked up. Seeing Oscar upset was like a literal punch to the gut. "If it was bad, we would have told you."

"But it wasn't good for you." Oscar shook his head.

I took a deep breath before speaking. "It was difficult doing the back-and-forth day and night shifts. But I appreciated the opportunity."

He nodded solemnly. "Speaking of opportunities, have you made any movement on your own business? I haven't spoken to you about it much lately, but please know that I want to help you in any way that you need."

"Thank you, Oscar. Um, well, I've put in an offer on the furniture store next door."

"The Schmidt's place?" Oscar asked, his eyes lighting up.

"That's the one!" I said brightly. "I'm waiting to hear from my realtor about it."

Oscar's eyes drew together in concern for a moment before he started to speak, but Donna came bursting back into the office.

"And another thing, Oscar- oh, hi peaches, how are you- Oscar, if he thinks he can come in here and spout all that nonsense-"

I slid out of Oscar's office around the angry Donna and went out to the store. I set my mug down at the register I typically used before going into the management office to get a cash drawer from Benjamin. He pulled one out of the front safe and handed it to me before I had even asked.

"Thank you, sir," I said brightly.

He quirked an eyebrow. "Save it for later," he said in a husky voice.

I snorted a laugh.

"Did Oscar get to tell you everything before Donna came in? I heard her screech from here," he said and leaned back in the creaking office chair. He twirled a pen between his long fingers.

"He said no more overnights, so that's cool," I said with a shrug.

"Yeah, and the staff meeting at three," Benjamin added.

"Oh, nope, he didn't get to that," I replied with a shrug. "What do you think it is?"

"He's just announcing that we're done doing overnights. He wanted to tell us first," Benjamin shrugged. "And likely the schedule for our winter season events."

"All we need is Santa breakfasts every weekend," I giggled. "Oscar is a great Santa."

"Uncanny," Benjamin agreed with a lopsided smile.

A customer called a polite "Hello?" from my register line and I hurried to open my drawer.

The day went as usual until we closed the store for one hour for our staff meeting at three. We all gathered in the staff room, talking amongst ourselves, until Oscar came out of his office with a stack of papers.

"Alright everyone, we've got a few things on the agenda today. First is our calendar of events for the winter. If you notice, we have quite a few," Oscar began. His mustache twitched excitedly as he handed out printed calendars. "We're going to add a few character events in. I'll be Santa again this year-" he paused and blushed as we cheered. "Yes, yes, thank you. I'll have elves with me, and I want to have a few Disney characters, as well. I'll let you all know who is cast for the events as we get closer. The cereal tasting event with the children went well, so I'm adding a soup tasting."

Everyone shuffled, and a few people groaned. I had not been at the cereal event, but I heard it was a mess. It wasn't difficult to imagine a few dozen children sloshing hot soup everywhere. I trusted Oscar to come up with something, so I kept my opinions to myself other than a quick glance at Benjamin. He was standing across the room from me, leaning against the cement wall with his arms crossed over his chest. Our quick eye contact portrayed both of our hesitance at the event and our amusement.

"We will also have a bake-off event, and a few wine tastings for the adults," Oscar finished his list. "It will be a busy, happy season. Speaking of happiness, I am happy to announce that both Layla and Benjamin will rejoin us every day. We will no longer be offering overnight hours as of today, and I have let the other overnight employees go."

I looked at Benjamin with raised eyebrows. He rolled his eyes and mouthed "stealing" to me. I grimaced in response. The surrounding murmuring covered our silent conversation.

"Both Layla and Benjamin have been here for years. Layla's been here for ten years and Benjamin for five. They have become so dear to me." Oscar stopped to swallow his emotion. I kept a soft smile on my face as everyone looked at us. Benjamin stood up from his leaning position and looked unsure of what was happening. "I am so proud of them. They both have dreams of owning their own businesses. Benjamin a tattoo shop and Layla a bookstore. In fact, they've both put in offers on the same location!" Oscar stopped to chuckle proudly.

He continued to speak, but I was no longer listening. My heart pounded in my chest, and I looked up to make eye contact with Benjamin again. His brows were drawn together, and his jaw clenched. We both stood, arms crossed and scowling at each other until the meeting ended. He needed to rescind his offer. That location was mine. He had known I was actively looking for a place for my bookstore. He hadn't even mentioned looking for a place for his tattoo shop. It felt like a personal betrayal rather than the coincidence that Oscar presented it as.

The meeting finished up not long after Oscar talked about a few other upcoming sales, town events, and staff vacations. I didn't listen to much more of what he said. My arms stayed crossed, and I knew I looked angry when Donna patted me on the elbow as she got up and left.

When we were alone in the room, we both stomped to meet each other face to face. I scowled up at him and he looked down at me with determination. "Withdraw your offer," I demanded at the same time he said, "Cancel it."

"No," we both replied simultaneously again.

He took a breath and shook his head at me.

"I'm not taking back my offer. I need that store," I insisted. "*You* take *yours* back."

"I'm not doing it. I put in an offer on that store as soon as I saw it. You don't even have your inventory yet. You can't even open," he fought.

"It doesn't matter! You knew I was looking for a place for my store and you never even talked about looking for a place," I argued in return. I glared up at him.

His jaw clenched as he glared back down at me. He was single-handedly blocking everything I'd worked for the last few years.

"That store is too big for what you need," he argued.

"No, it's perfect. I'll be able to do a lounge area and have a stage," I replied.

He shook his head again and exhaled harshly before stepping away from me. He turned around and put his hands flat against the staff room table. Benjamin wasn't giving in and the indignant anger in me rose.

"I- I'm not coming over tonight. It seems like we may not be... compatible anymore," I said harshly, but my voice trembled in the end.

He spun to face me quickly, and I saw the hurt and confusion flicker over his eyes. I gnashed my teeth. His being hurt fixed nothing. He was still trying to ruin my chance at owning my bookstore. "Fine. If that's what you think," he ground out and turned back around.

"Fine," I parroted.

We stood silently and angrily breathed for a moment before I spun and stomped through the staff doors.

I spent the rest of my shift so angry I was near tears. It didn't feel fair. Benjamin's bid on the store and his refusal to back down made me think we could never come to an agreement in a relationship. It wasn't worth it to try anything together. That realization was like a punch to the gut. It had felt like something was finally about to click with him and I. And now we were back to nothing. Coworkers.

That evening I got a call from Susan about my offer on the store. The Schmidt's wanted to meet with their family before they decided, and I would hear about their verdict on Monday morning. It wasn't more than a weekend, but it felt like forever.

Benjamin and I didn't speak the rest of the week. We both still had the same working schedule, and we finished our Friday shift in silence and didn't talk on our day off on Saturday. Part of me wanted to reach out and touch him. The other part wanted to scream at him. I'd spent my evening trying to read to keep myself distracted, but nothing held my attention. At midnight on Saturday, I was staring a hole in my phone, wanting to get a message from him. I knew it was selfish. I knew it was silly. But I couldn't help the ache in my belly. I knew it was selfish to want him to lose the store and then come back to me. It would only lead to resentment if I got the store, and he didn't, and we kept seeing each other. I knew I wouldn't be able to forget it if it was reversed.

The leap in my stomach when my phone lit up with a message solidified the intensity of my feelings for Benjamin. My body had a physical reaction to the prospect of talking to him. I was in love with Benjamin.

I was in love with Benjamin.

But he wasn't in love with me. Not enough.

17

I picked up my phone and read the message. "I don't want to talk. I don't want to make plans. Not right now. Right now, all I can think about is how touching you made me feel. Fuck, Layla. We never talked about deep stuff, but fuck, I'll just say it. You think I flirt with everyone and, yeah, I guess I do. I turn people's thoughts away from me and back to themselves. I have control over them and their feelings and their thoughts. It's crazy but I need that control over people. I have to control the narrative until I get to know someone. And you're the first person to literally and figuratively hand me the knife- the control. What we had in the stupid gazebo was the best experience of my life. I don't think I've ever felt that relaxed before. And *you* trusted me. *You* gave me that control willingly."

A few seconds after I opened the message, the three dots showing he was typing appeared.

"You're awake. You read it."

"I couldn't sleep," I replied.

"You replied."

"I did."

"Can I see you?" he asked.

"You said you didn't want to talk."

"I don't."

"Is this a booty call?" I questioned, not entirely against the idea. My girlboss feminism dissipated as the horniness increased. I closed my phone and my eyes and took a few steadying breaths.

I was alone in this world. I had no family and only a few friends. Every aspect of my life was controlled by me. As a result, I spent a considerable amount of time only trusting myself, and it had been a bit of a relief of that burden to let go. The release of tension in my body was noticeable after our last hook up, but I had attributed it to multiple orgasms. I hadn't considered it was letting go of control and *trusting* Benjamin that had relaxed me. I hadn't allowed myself to think much about what I was losing by ending things with Benjamin. His text showed me I really didn't know *who* I would miss by ending it. I didn't truly know Benjamin. But I knew how he made me feel. I sighed and opened my eyes to see his response.

This wasn't choosing a man over my goals. This was enjoying our bodies and how we made each other feel before we made any decisions about our stores. I wasn't giving up. I wasn't backing down. Neither was he. But I understood what he was saying about control and I wanted the same things.

"Yes."

"Where?" I asked probably too quickly to keep my feminist card.

"I'm outside your building, buzz me in," he replied just as quickly.

"No talking? No compromises and bargaining?"

"None."

I considered telling him to give me a few minutes to light a candle, clean up my takeout boxes, and change my sheets. But that was too close to romance. This was just meeting a need. I was wearing a pair of little cotton pajama shorts and a baggy t-shirt from a previous Oscar's store event. I stood at the front door of my apartment and pressed the button that let him into the building. Peeking through the peephole, I saw him approach in the slightly fish eyed view. He was wearing his leather jacket over a white t-shirt and jeans. His hair looked like he'd been running his hands through it for hours.

He smirked at the peephole. "Let me in, little one, or I'll huff and I'll puff." He was grinning but his tone sent shivers of anticipation down my spine.

"How'd you know where I live?" I asked through the door.

"I have access to every employee's home address," he said. "I looked it up."

I rolled my eyes and opened the door, stepping back to look at him. A gust of wind from the hall whirled in, bringing in his scent and the scent of decaying leaves. I breathed deeply and evenly as we stared at each other.

He snapped into action after a sweep of his gaze. He stepped in and kicked the door closed behind him and crowded me against my kitchen table. It screeched as I moved it backwards and a chair fell over on the other side. I gasped at the clatter and looked down at my almost cowering body. My shoulders were rounded in, and I was practically hyperventilating. Benjamin gripped my jaw where it met my neck with a large, warm hand and forced me to look up at him. His brown eyes met mine, and I saw the intensity and desperation there. For someone who talked a lot, he communicated the important things best with his body. His jaw clenched as he breathed me in.

"Can I play?" he asked, his voice low and gravelly.

I swallowed and paused. Those same animal instincts returned. The one that said to run and the one that said to submit to him.

"Will you hurt me?" I asked in a whisper.

His eyes flickered with concern before he replied, "No, little one. Nothing more than you can handle. But we're new to this, so we need limits. We'll go old school for safety and say red for stop, yellow for slow down or change something, and green for keep going."

I nodded in understanding.

"Are you ready?" he asked, pressing his body into mine and moving his thumb to press into my mouth.

I licked the tip of his thumb and felt his hardening dick jump in his jeans. "Will you fuck me?"

"If you're a good girl," he said, his voice low but soothing. "So, can I play?"

"Yes," I whispered hoarsely.

An intimidating smile curled the corners of his lips and his eyes darkened. "Good," he said simply before grabbing me by my shoulders and spinning me around. He shoved me down to bend over the table, my cheek pressed against the cool wood. Maybe I should have tidied. Crumbs from my breakfast toast pressed into my cheek. My muscles were stiff and bunched in defense against him, and I took a steadying breath and worked on relaxing my muscles. I listened as he shrugged off his leather jacket.

"Wait, no keep it on," I said and lifted my head. He was carefully hanging it on my coat rack and toeing off his black boots.

He smirked over at me. "Your apartment is hot as fuck."

"I like it cozy," I defended and pushed up from my position.

His eyes flashed. "Put your face back down on the table."

I obeyed, and he approached me swiftly and yanked down my cotton shorts. My knees knocked together involuntarily. He made a sound of disapproval and landed a hard smack on my right ass cheek. I gasped in shock and pain. I was wearing a pair of cheeky panties that had ridden up and were now more like a thong. His teeth sunk into the globe of my ass, and I hissed a breath between my teeth.

"This ass," he said reverently and grabbed two handfuls of flesh. He kneaded my flesh and then stood up.

Benjamin spun me around and lifted me so my legs wrapped around his waist. His lips met mine in a searing kiss that was sure to leave me wet and panting. He walked down the hall and opened the first door. It was my coat closet. I giggled as he closed it and moved to the second door. He opened that one and saw that it was my linen closet. I giggled again as he pulled his lips from mine with a huff.

"Bed," he demanded. "Before I fuck you in the coat closet. I don't particularly care."

I pointed behind us to the door across the hall. It was mostly ajar, as I hadn't closed it before meeting him, but my room was dark, save the warm fairy lights I had strung up above my bed. He kicked the door open the rest of the way and carried me to my bed. He threw me down onto the unmade blankets with a bounce.

Benjamin looked around for a moment before his eyes landed on my bathrobe strewn over the storage trunk at the end of my bed. He pulled the belt from the loops and converged on me almost viciously. I let him tie my hands with the terry cloth belt to my painted iron headboard. My adrenaline matched my lust, and I panted as I watched him pull a sheathed knife out of his pocket. He opened the clasp of the sheath and slid the knife out slowly. The metal was shining and clean. It was a different knife than the one he'd had before.

"Pretty," I said.

"It'll be prettier when it cuts you," he said simply as if he was discussing the weather.

My heart rate kicked up even more as he stared at me, tied up while he held a knife. This wasn't safe. He could get too carried away and hurt me. He probably didn't know what he was doing. But the fear and lust combination had me wetter than I'd ever been. Benjamin was a safe person. I was safe. If he went too far, my phone was right there on the nightstand to call for help. If I could call at all being tied up.

"You should be afraid of me," he breathed.

"I am," my whisper almost whistled with how dry my throat was.

He smirked. "This blade was in my car all evening, so it's a bit cold." He crawled onto the bed and kneeled between my legs. "We should probably warm it up."

He lifted my shirt up to my neck and slid the flat side of the dagger against the soft skin of my stomach. It felt like a cold scratch and goosebumps rose in its wake. He smirked at the raised skin and then lowered his face so his tongue could follow the same path. I sighed and closed my eyes.

"Does it feel cold?" he asked as he traced it over my side.

The sensation of the knife was between a tickle and a scratch along the sensitive skin on my ribcage. "Yes," I breathed as his tongue followed the knife.

He drew the knife below my ribcage at my sternum. He paused there before moving on to my other side to draw the knife back down towards my belly to mirror the other side. His mouth kissed and licked my skin after the knife.

The knife remained cool, though warmer than before, as it drew across my skin. I was acutely aware of where it was on my body. My animal brain recognized the threat and had me on full alert. When his warm, wet tongue followed the knife, the other part of me that was all hormones shivered. He didn't cut me, only drew the knife along my skin until my body stopped reacting the same way. Once my skin stopped raising in goosebumps, he changed tactics. He cut my panties off of me with a quick tug that had me bouncing back onto the bed. I squealed at the quick aggression.

He sat back on his heels and examined my body. I was still wearing my old t-shirt and his eyes glinted as he considered it and my bound hands. He took the knife in one hand and the collar of my shirt in the other and cut through from the top to the bottom. He was careful, being near my face and neck, but as he got closer to the bottom, the pull of the knife became almost vicious. I bounced again as the knife broke through the bottom hem. He pushed the two halves of my shirt open so I was bared to him.

He hadn't seen me naked yet and his eyes drank me in. I blushed and tried to close my legs while sucking in my stomach. He batted my knees open with a fleeting annoyed expression. Keeping his hands just above my knees, he slid his body down so he was lying on his stomach between my legs. My blush deepened when I realized he was staring at my pussy. I was thankful for the dim lighting at that moment.

"Is this for me?" he asked as he lightly traced one finger in the wetness gathered.

I was intensely aware of my body after the knife was on my skin. I gasped at his feather light touch.

"Is it?" he asked again and popped his finger in his mouth as if he was tasting a dessert.

"Yes," I whispered.

"Hmm," he hummed, considering. "I know we talked about your heart being mine. But *this* is what I want right now." He licked a soft, wet line over my folds.

I squealed, and my thighs trembled.

"Is this pussy mine?" he asked in a gravelly whisper that ghosted hot air over my sex.

"Yes," I repeated in a whine, desperate for actual contact. I strained against the terry cloth at my wrists.

Benjamin shuffled up and put his elbows on either side of my thighs, holding my legs down with his weight. He picked the knife up from the bed and poised it just above where my pubic hair would grow if I hadn't shaved. He looked up at me to gauge my feelings before he carved a quick line. I hissed in a breath through my teeth.

"Color," he demanded, his voice hard.

It took me a moment to understand. "Oh, uh, green."

He took a second before returning the knife to my skin and carving something curved. I couldn't tell what he was doing because my eyes had fallen shut.

He paused another second, and I thought he was waiting for my color response. "Lime."

"What?"

"Lime. It's green but close to yellow," I explained breathlessly.

He snorted a laugh. "That's not... I mean, I guess it's helpful to be accurate."

Benjamin looked down. There was a nickel sized pool of blood. He licked it up and my nerve endings got confused. My pussy clenched as if he had just licked there instead of the cut. I felt a gush of arousal and he looked down at it. He cursed and reached a hand down to adjust himself before returning to his artwork.

He carved one more curve, and I cried out and strained against the ties. A tear rolled down into the hair at my temple.

"Color, baby. Color," he said urgently and sat up.

"Macaroni and cheese," I gasped.

"What the fu- oh, orange, yellow with a little red. Fucking hell, Layla," he groaned and then chuckled. "I'm done anyway. You're marked."

"Marked?" I asked and looked down at my body.

"Claimed," he said as if it was clarification. He stooped down and licked over the forming blood again, and my jumbled nerve endings and adrenaline sent another wave of pleasure over my body. Once the blood was cleared, I saw a small capital B just above my mound.

"You'll carve your initial into me, but you won't tattoo me?" I asked breathlessly.

He frowned for a moment before keeping a thoughtful expression on his face as he scooted down and licked over my pussy again. I cried out and arched off of the mattress. "Yup," he said finally after a few more long licks.

I shook my head against the pillow and scoffed.

The scoff got stuck in my throat because his tongue dove through my folds and into my opening. I fought back a scream as he devoured me, his hands gripping my trembling thighs. It didn't take long before I was coming with a shout of his name.

"That's it, good girl," he soothed as he caressed my thighs. "You did so good letting me carve you up and coming on my mouth. I love to see you dripping all over your sheets. Blood and come. So fucking perfect."

"Let me touch you," I said desperately. He had made me come, and I wanted to return the favor. I wanted him to feel as good as I did.

"No," he said, and his eyes flashed menacingly. He rose from the bed and quickly stripped off his clothes. I stared as he bared his skin to me. My mouth watered at the sight of all of his muscles and smooth tattooed skin.

"Why not?" I asked, and stared longingly at his muscular body.

He stroked himself a few times as he turned back towards me. "Because I said," he said gruffly as he got back onto the bed and took his place between my legs again.

I shivered with anticipation now that we were here. My core rushed with arousal, and I bit my lip as I watched him kneel in front of me.

"Are you on the pill?" he asked as he lined himself up at my entrance.

"No, IUD," I said eagerly, realizing that he meant to fuck me.

He surged forward and entered me in one harsh thrust. I was surely wet enough that he met no resistance.

"Fucking hell," he groaned and buried his face in my neck. He didn't move, letting me get used to the size and weight of him inside me.

I wasn't able to hold him with my hands, so I wrapped my legs around his hips as I pushed up against him.

"You feel amazing," he moaned in a deep voice in my ear. "Oh, fuck. I've wanted to be inside of you for so long."

"And I've wanted you inside me for even longer," I breathed and tried to roll my hips under him to get him moving.

"Hold on," he chuckled and pressed a large hand against my hip to settle me. "Give me a second. Your pussy is so fucking perfect I'm about to blow already."

I held still semi patiently. I licked across his broad shoulder, as it was all I could do being tied up. His muscles quivered, and I smiled. He moaned into my neck before I bit down on his shoulder. He grunted before pushing up on his hands. "Alright, little one, you asked for it."

I was smiling because I had, indeed, asked for it. I didn't know *what* I had asked for, though. He pulled out and then slammed back into me so hard I shifted up the mattress. I was gasping with each thrust as he grunted over me. The top of my head hit my headboard, and he wrapped a hand around my neck to keep me still and use it as leverage in his punishing thrusts. He stopped to sling my legs over his shoulders before folding me so he could still choke me. I yelled out my pain as he hit my cervix with a thrust. He shifted back a little, so he didn't go as deep.

"You take me so well," he groaned. "You take all of me so well. What a good fucking pussy."

His voice was strained and deep. A crimson flush covered his entire chest and neck. I was happy to finally see how much of him glowed when he blushed. He sat up, my legs still over his shoulders and his hands on my thighs as he fucked me into the mattress. His head tipped back with a moan, exposing his throat to me. It was the hottest thing I had ever seen, and it set off my second orgasm of the night. I rolled my hips and my eyes squeezed closed.

When I opened my eyes, his abs were wet, and his eyes were blazing on me. "Oh, fuck," I said, shocked.

He gave me a panting grin and three more hard thrusts before he fell forward, his lips on my neck, as he came with a shout. He shuddered and pushed even further into me as he came. When he was done, he rolled off of me and reached up to untie my hands.

In the post orgasm glow, I wanted to cuddle. I reached for him, but he was already getting up. He slipped on his underwear and jeans before turning back to me. His face was clouded and his jaw clenched. I remembered his text. This was just sex. Just an exchange of control.

"Layla," he started.

"It's okay, I know this was just sex," I said and pulled the covers over my body and sat up.

He swallowed and nodded; his jaw still clenched. He was beautiful and I wanted him. I wanted the initial on my body and the healing X over my heart to mean something without giving up my own goals. My chest ached looking at him. I turned away from him, my legs hanging off the other side of the bed.

"You can go. I'll see you in the morning," I said, trying to sound casual.

I heard the soft slide of his t-shirt being put back on. He picked up the knife and I heard him wipe it on the textured fabric of his jeans, the tip catching on the seam before he sheathed it.

"Lock the door after me," he murmured.

I nodded.

He left the room, stopping to get his shoes and jacket back on. I heard the front door click shut behind him and I let out a shuddering sob.

I had thought that sex would be enough with Benjamin. Sex and the exchange of control. While last time I had felt relaxed and satiated after, this time I felt like I was still in danger. I felt like I was about to lose everything I had worked for- the store and Benjamin. Something was missing this time. To convince myself that I was safe, I shuffled to the front door and locked it before heading into the shower.

The soap burned the carved B. I treated it with antiseptic and covered it with a bandage. Angrily, I stripped my sheets from my bed, throwing my blood and come covered linens into the washer. I didn't have the energy to make the bed, so I crashed onto the couch and slept fitfully until my morning alarm.

18

As soon as I got to work in the morning, Donna cornered me. She had a mischievous glint in her eyes and my stomach dropped. She either knew something about me and Benjamin, or Oscar had a surprise event today. And I was not in the mood for either.

"Hey peaches," she greeted me.

"Hey, Donna," I replied as I shut my locker.

"Dan was at Scoot's last night," she said and raised her eyebrows at me.

"Dan?" I asked, searching my memory for someone named Dan.

"Officer Dan, only he was off duty when he was at Scoot's," she explained with a dismissive wave.

My stomach clenched. "Oh, yeah?" I tried to be casual. "That's nice."

"Said he caught you and *Benjamin* kissing at the gazebo," she said in a normal tone, but her eyes told me she was screaming internally.

"Is that what he said?" I said, and a blush rose to my cheeks.

"Is it true? Oh, please tell me it's true!" she practically screeched. Her smoker's voice didn't allow her to squeal like an excited girl anymore. It came out like a strangled cat.

I looked down as I tied my apron strings. I nodded while keeping my eyes on my sneakers.

"*What*?!" she screeched. "And you didn't tell me?"

I shook my head and gave her a sad little smile. "No, it's... nothing."

"You and Benjamin making out at the gazebo in the middle of the night is not *nothing*! I've been trying to get you two together for years!" she insisted excitedly.

"No, I mean, there's nothing between us. We have... different goals for our futures," I explained, and clocked in.

Donna wasn't having it. "No, the problem is that you two have too similar goals. You're competing for the same storefront, for goodness' sake," she said and scoffed. "You should just share the space. One side your books and the other side his tattoos."

I didn't reply, thinking about what she said. It was kind of ridiculous, but I kind of liked it.

"You may not see it, but I think you two work well together. Hell, you're the only ones to survive the entire summer doing overnight shifts. Unless you two were..." she trailed off suggestively.

"No, Donna, we weren't," I partially lied. There *had* been that one time. And a half.

"Oh well," she said and shrugged disappointedly as we both entered the store through the swinging doors.

It was a busy Sunday morning, and the flow of customers remained heavy throughout the day. I knew Benjamin was there;

he was the one who answered my call when I needed a rain check at the register. We didn't talk during the day except for quick work-related things. And even then his eyes were heavy on me.

As I was coming back from my lunch, there was a store announcement. "Layla, clean up on aisle five. Layla Avery, clean up on aisle five." It was Benjamin's voice, and I scowled. I was on register today, not store support. But I grabbed the broom and dustbin and headed to the baking aisle.

There were no obvious spills. No flour or sugar bags on the floor. I looked around and didn't see a single thing out of place. There were a few customers shopping in the aisle and they shrugged at me as I looked around. This was the aisle Benjamin and I had hooked up in. My face remained in a scowl as I walked up and down the aisle, looking closely at the shelves. Maybe someone had knocked over a row of something on the shelf. Just as I was about to leave the aisle, something hot pink caught my eye. It was in the same section of shelving that Benjamin and I had leaned against. There, sitting on the shelf, just behind the stack of frosting cans, were my panties. The hot pink cheeky panties that he had cut off of me last night. I swiped them up and shoved them into my apron pocket. Looking around frantically, I saw that nobody had noticed me.

Cheeks blazing, I stomped to where Benjamin was leaning against the front manager's office door. He was smirking at me, and I pushed him into the room and shut the door behind me. All the nosy onlooking customers (and Donna) could suck it.

I pulled the ruined panties out of my apron pocket and waved them in his face. "What the hell, Benjamin?" I hissed.

"Meet me after work," he said instead of answering, his smirk still in place.

I sighed and looked down, feeling sadness and shame creep up again. "No."

"Not a booty call," he clarified and touched my arm.

"Then what?" I asked, looking at him now.

He looked earnest and kind. "We need to have that talk."

"I don't think that's a good idea." I shook my head. Having a conversation about how we'd never make it other than a kinky hook up link was not a conversation I wanted to have.

"We need to work something out. This is-" he stopped to grab my chin to keep me looking at him. "This is bigger than just the store. I think you know that."

I shifted on my feet. "Okay, let's talk."

"Tonight, at my place. I'll even cook for you." He grinned and let go of my chin.

"I believe I had been previously promised steak," I joked quietly and hesitantly agreeing.

"You got it," he agreed cheerfully before he opened the door and gestured for me to leave. "Oh, and look angry when you leave so all the customers don't think I just bent you over the desk and fucked you."

"I've been in here all of thirty seconds," I laughed.

"Not everyone in this town knows about my skill set in the bedroom," he said with fake insult.

I crossed my arms over my chest and stomped out of the office with a scowling pout. When everyone saw I didn't appear ravaged, they returned to their shopping and ringing. They all thought they had front row seats to fresh gossip. I glanced at

Donna who was grinning slyly at me from her register and rolled my eyes.

After work, Benjamin had me get into his car instead of my own. He put two bags of groceries in the trunk and got in the driver's seat. "What a busy day," he commented as he started the car.

I opened my mouth to reply, but was interrupted by a blast of incredibly loud rock music. Benjamin jumped to turn the volume down. "Sorry," he said sheepishly. "I was feeling angsty this morning."

We chatted easily about music until we got to Benjamin's townhouse. His landscaping was basic but well maintained. Likely managed by the company that owned the property. Benjamin parked in the numbered spot right in front of his townhouse and he gathered the groceries from the trunk. He opened the front door and let me in first.

His entryway had a pile of shoes and a pile of coats on the floor. The walls were beige and scuffed near the shoe pile. It was a clean space otherwise. He toed off his shoes and walked to the kitchen. I followed suit. His kitchen was clean other than a few dishes in the sink and an almost full garbage can. He was a tidy person, if not minimalistic. A fruit bowl sat on the counter, but it was filled with baked goods in their plastic containers. I smiled at it. Benjamin opened his fridge and put away the groceries. He had a decent amount of food already in the fridge and I realized I had been expecting take-out containers and maybe one bottle of ketchup.

"Do you like red wine?" he asked as he rummaged through a drawer and pulled out a corkscrew.

"Yeah," I said and continued to watch him in nervous silence.

"Okay good, because I think we need it," he chuckled as he poured me a glass. It was a heavy pour, and I made a mental note to sip it slowly.

Benjamin poured his own glass and held it out. "To compromises and thoroughly sanitized knives."

"Cheers," I giggled and knocked my glass against his.

"Sláinte," he said, and we both took sips of our wine.

We were silent as he took out the ingredients for dinner.

"So, our compromise..." I said and sat at his small kitchen table. There were no toast crumbs on his table like there were on mine. I ran my hands over the smooth cherry wood. Only one ring of a water stain marred the otherwise clean table.

"No," he said and turned around, pointing at me with a chef's knife. His lips were curled up at the corners in a smile. "Not until we've eaten."

"Okay, okay," I giggled. "Well, do you need any help?"

"Hm, you can make the salad. I just put the spinach in the fridge," he said as I approached. "Thinly slice some of that red onion, quarter those grape tomatoes, and there's a seed mix in the cabinet on the right. Oh, and crumble some of that goat cheese on top. I'll make the dressing."

"What?!" I had heard everything he said, but I was shocked that he was the one saying it.

"I like food and cooking," he said with a grin. "For a while I thought maybe I'd be a chef. I took some culinary classes in high school but ended up really falling in love with tattooing."

"That's really cool," I said thoughtfully as I followed the directions I had been given.

"Did you always want to open a bookstore?" he asked as I was slicing the onions. He was cutting baby potatoes in half and putting them in a roasting pan.

"No. I didn't know what I wanted for a very long time. It was only a few years ago that I figured it out. I kind of figured I'd just be working at Oscar's forever," I replied. Then I thought better of it and snapped, "That's not to say I want the store less than you do."

"Put your claws away, kitty," he teased in a deep tone. "I wasn't going to say anything like that."

"Sorry," I apologized with a sigh.

"I don't have you here tonight to trick you or take anything from you," he assured me as he drizzled olive oil over the potatoes. He dropped in a few spices and salt, but his labels were handwritten in sharpie on the bottles, and I couldn't read them.

I finished making the salad and took my wine to the table. Benjamin moved about his kitchen with a grace reserved for dancers. His movements were precise and intentional. I hoped he'd cook the steaks shirtless so I could watch his muscles move and tattoos dance. The steaks had been sitting on the counter on a plate and were now seasoned and set gently in a sizzling pan of melted butter and a few sprigs of fresh thyme. I watched in awe as he cooked. His brows furrowed in concentration and as he spooned butter over the steak as it cooked. My stomach rumbled. I moaned at the smell. "It smells so good."

He glanced up at me and gave a smile. "It will taste even better."

Looking down, I realized I had finished my glass of wine. Watching Benjamin cook had made me thirsty. He plated the steaks and potatoes on dark gray ceramic plates, topped up our wine, and had me set the table. The food looked incredible, and he waited for me to take the first bite. It was delicious, and I was sure my loud moan and closed eyes told him how much I thought so.

He was grinning when my eyes opened again, and he was taking his first bite. He appeared proud of himself as we ate mostly in silence. I felt his gaze on me whenever my eyes were not on him. I knew so little about him but felt a connection to him on a deeper level than his favorite color and childhood pet's name. Last night this man had been in my apartment- had been inside *me*- and now here I was having an awkward dinner with him. I allowed him to tie me up and carve his initial into my flesh, but I couldn't bring myself to speak tonight.

When he finished his food, he sat back and watched me take my last few bites. "So, tell me, if the whole fiasco with our stores didn't exist, where would we be right now?"

I wiped my mouth with my napkin and took the last sip of my wine. I looked him directly in the eye and said, "In bed."

He smirked. "Right. Let's forget the store stuff for a minute. I told you I thought this was bigger than that and I wasn't joking." As he spoke, his expression morphed from his smirk to a serious, intense gaze.

"What do you mean by that?" I asked, feeling self-conscious. There was a possibility that he didn't mean that he was feeling the same connection as I was. I wasn't about to make a fool out of myself in front of someone I was technically competing against.

"Layla, you let me carve into your skin. You let me tie you up." He leaned forward and tried to smother the intensity in his voice. He took a deep breath. "I told you I needed control to feel comfortable. You're the first person to let me have that control during sex."

"You've never carved your initials into someone's flesh before?" I asked with a laugh.

"No."

"You're a tattoo artist."

"It's a bit different," he understated.

"How?"

"Cutting you was... intimate," he replied.

"Tattooing isn't intimate?" I asked.

"Not in the same way, no."

"Then why don't you tattoo girlfriends?" I asked, intrigued now.

"It's my artwork they'd be carrying around with them forever," he said.

"Well, I'll be carrying around the B you carved on me forever," I retorted.

He stared at me for a long moment. "I intend to be around just as long."

Shame and anger flashed through me, encouraged by the wine. "Why? Because I let you take control in bed?"

"No! I didn't finish," he said quickly to settle me. He took a breath before continuing. "You *let* me have control. You showed me you trusted me. You could have said all day long that you trusted me, but I wouldn't have believed you. I guess I needed to see it to believe it. When you let me have control, you accepted me. *All* of me. You didn't flinch. And we hardly know each other, really. Yeah, we've worked together for a couple of years, but it's not like we ever had any heart to hearts."

"What is there to flinch at?" I asked. "It's not like you're a criminal or something. You're Benjamin, you work at Oscar's, you love chocolate in your coffee, peanut butter bars, and slicing up girls."

He chuckled. "I have a hard time trusting people and I get a bit intense."

"I'm alone in the world and am pretty even keeled," I replied.

"A perfect victim," he said and let out a villainous laugh. I rolled my eyes.

"How do you have trust issues but yet work for Oscar? He puts us up to the weirdest stuff sometimes. It takes a lot of trust to give him the reins and your clothing sizes," I said with a smile.

"I trust Oscar." Benjamin nodded.

I gasped and put a hand to my chest. "Where is his B?"

He realized what I meant, and his head tilted back with a laugh. His real one. When we calmed down, he said more seriously, "Actually, you're the first person I've cut. You had me read that one book and I did some research afterward."

"I turned you on to a new kink?" I asked, shocked.

"Uh, yeah," he said and smiled.

"Have you tied girls up before?" I asked.

"Women, not girls, and yes," he clarified.

"Was it not enough?"

"They didn't like it," he answered. "And if they weren't totally into it and were too stiff, then it felt like lying. I couldn't trust them."

"I wasn't too stiff?" I asked.

"No, you were not," he said, his eyes simmering.

"Do you have to control everything? Like not just in the bedroom?" I asked quietly. I should have asked earlier. This was a huge deal breaker.

"No! No, I do like having control in the bedroom, but if I always have it, then it gets boring, you know? It gets stale. And not outside of sex. I'm not a controlling asshole, I promise. A relationship with me is a partnership," he said adamantly.

"And girls- sorry, *women*- telling you in other ways that they trusted you didn't do the trick?"

"No, it always felt like a lie. I needed cold hard facts, I guess," he said with a shrug.

I considered for a moment before I spoke again. "I wasn't kidding when I said I was alone in this world. Not just this town. It's only me. I've had to have full control of my entire life for a long time. It felt... amazing to let some of that control fall away for a little while." I looked at him from under my lashes. His gaze went from simmering with lust to care and understanding. He reached for my hand on the table. I let him envelop my hand in his. "We complement each other," I added.

He looked confused for a second. "You're very beautiful."

"Uh, thanks. Wait, *complement*, not compliment," I burst into a fit of giggles.

"You're literally saying the same word," he said confusedly.

"Complement with an *e* means things go together or add to each other," I giggled.

"Alright, Hermione," he said with a smile.

"If I'm Hermione, you're definitely Draco," I said as my giggles died down.

He considered for a moment. "Eh, he was a pussy. I'm Neville with the sword at the end."

"If you say so," I said.

We smiled at each other for a few moments before I looked away. "Speaking of complementing each other, Donna made a suggestion today."

"Oh?" he said warily. He had a point; Donna was a spirited individual and nobody ever knew what was next with her.

"Yeah, she suggested we both own the store together. Books on one side and tattoos on the other," I said hesitantly.

Benjamin was silent as he stared at me.

"We don't have to, I mean, it's silly. It was just something Donna said and-"

"What do you think?" he asked and gripped my hand again. "Honestly, I want to know what you think about it."

"I think it could be really good," I whispered, looking at his tattooed hand wrapped around my unmarked one.

"No, tell me what you think, Layla," he insisted.

"It would be amazing. You could do bookish themed tattoos for people and suggest books when you're talking while you tattoo them. We could have the café in the middle, and the outgoing inked up people can mingle with the shy bookworms," I listed more confidently and looked at him in his warm brown eyes.

"You know, people with tattoos aren't always more outgoing and bookworms aren't always shy," he smiled.

"I guess I just pictured more you's and more me's meeting." I shrugged.

"The mixers would be awesome," he said.

"We could offer discounts for books if you get a tattoo," I added.

"We can have a battle of the inks game nights," he said excitedly.

"We can take part in whatever nonsense Oscar has going on," I said with a laugh.

"We can outdo his parade floats," Benjamin laughed with me.

"We could stay together," I whispered, my heart pounding in my chest. It felt like my entire body was screaming for this to be true. I was at the edge of my seat, my hand in Benjamin's was slick with sweat, and my breathing rapid.

19

"We could stay together," he repeated back to me. His eyes on mine blazed with heat and I almost gasped at the intensity I saw there.

Benjamin stood up from his seat so fast the chair tipped back and knocked onto the floor. He reached across the table to me, knocking my empty wineglass to the floor where it shattered. I stood up as he grabbed me by the back of my head. He pulled me towards him and kissed me fiercely. I squeaked in shock against his lips, but opened my mouth to him. His kiss was ferocious and full of need. It differed from our previous kisses because he let my tongue dominate. He let me guide the kiss. And I guided it around the table and to where I assumed was his living room. I was just about to push him onto the couch when he stopped me.

"Bed," he demanded. "Not my new couch."

I snorted. "Good thinking."

He led me by the hand down a short hallway to his bedroom. His walls were a dark gray and only one black-and-white photo of a vintage tattoo parlor hung on the walls. A full-length mirror leaned against the wall near his door and his bed was unmade. It was much less tidy than his kitchen with clothes strewn all over the floor.

"Didn't clean up for me?" I teased.

"Are you kidding? I'm pretty sure I fucked you next to pizza crust in your bed last night," he retorted as he sat on the end of his bed. He pulled me to stand between his legs.

I scoffed, "That's an exaggeration."

He only smiled and lifted my shirt over my head. We were in our work clothes. I was wearing my logo polo, and he was still in his button down. He trailed his fingers down my sides and leaned over to kiss the soft flesh of my stomach. His kisses over my skin were soft and reverent now as he reached around me and unhooked my bra. With him sitting on the bed, his head was only an inch or two below my eye level, and I watched the blaze in his eyes smolder as he looked at my breasts. He stared at them, his hands twitching on my ribcage.

"What?" I asked quietly.

"I haven't seen your tits yet. I'm admiring them," he said in a hushed, serious voice.

"You saw them last night," I reminded him.

"I did?" he asked and looked up at me, shock on his face.

"I guess maybe not, but my tits were definitely out. You cut my Oscar's Groceries 2019 rib roast t-shirt right off of me," I reminded him.

"Hm," he said with his lips pulled down in a frown and his eyebrows up. "I remember doing that, but I think I was more focused on... this." He lowered his gaze and his hands to the button on my khakis.

"I'd say," I scoffed.

He rolled his eyes and gently peeled my pants over my legs. I stepped out of them, my hands on his strong, warm shoulders. The heat emanating through the worn cotton of his button down was almost feverish. It reminded me he was still fully clothed. When my pants were off and Benjamin sat back up and looked at me, I pushed on his chest so he fell back on the bed. He smirked up at me as I straddled him at his waist and slowly unbuttoned his shirt. I unbuttoned from the bottom up, licking and kissing and nipping at the skin I uncovered. He was panting and hard beneath me when I reached his neck. He gasped when I bit at the angle of his jaw and he clenched his hands in the rumpled bed sheets. I sat up and he curled up just enough to rip the shirt off the rest of the way. I fixed my eyes on his abs as he partially sat up and I dove to trace my tongue in the grooves of muscle definition. He realized what I was doing and held the crunch until his muscles quivered and he was chuckling through the strain.

"Aw, poor baby can't flex any longer?" I teased, looking up at him from under my lashes.

He growled deep in his chest and flipped us over, so he was looming over me. His smirk was still in place but didn't turn to that devilish grin I had come to expect. This was just silly, naughty Benjamin. My heart flipped in my chest and then sunk to my clit as he slid my last remaining article of clothing down my legs. He crawled back up and laid down next to me to kiss me long and sweet. I slung a leg over his still khaki clad hip and buried my hands in his loose blonde curls.

We kissed for a long time. Our mouths, tongues, and hands exploring each other's bodies softly and curiously. Compared to our previous encounters, it was almost innocent. It was a total change of pace, but it felt almost more important than our first kiss. At some point, he took off his pants and boxers without removing his lips from mine. Our fingers traced over our bodies, raising goosebumps on each other's skin as we went. We tangled together, his hard length pressed against my stomach, the coarse hair on his legs tickling the smooth skin of mine, and his skin scorching where we connected.

I opened my eyes to look at him, even though we were kissing. His eyes were closed, and his golden-brown lashes splayed over his relaxed cheeks. His brow was relaxed, too, and I remembered back to our last few encounters and realized he had been furrowed and creased. He was peaceful now as he kissed me. I smiled into our kiss and closed my eyes again.

As much as I loved kissing him and touching him, I was growing impatient. The sticky moisture against my stomach that had beaded from his cock matched the arousal spreading between my thighs. I decided it was up to me to make the first move. I reached a hand down to wrap around his length and he gasped, almost startled. His hips jerked forward as I stroked him. I broke the kiss to look down at what I was doing. My mouth watered, and I decided I needed a taste. He shifted so he was on his back on the bed. I crawled over him, not taking my hands off of him.

The sight of him with his head thrown back, his tattooed jaw and neck stretched as he moaned when I took him all the way in my mouth was enough to get my arousal dripping down my thighs.

"Fucking hell, Layla," he groaned, and his hands fisted in my hair.

I hummed around him, and he hissed in a breath through his teeth. "That *mouth*, little one. That *fucking* mouth."

I worked him slowly, wetly, alternating between soft and strong sucks. A sweat broke out over his skin as he involuntarily rolled his hips. Taking him all the way in, I sucked softly until he was in too far to continue to suck. His cock blocked my airway, and I held that position, watching transfixed as sweat trailed down his heaving, tattooed chest. The swirling designs quivering as he shook. As I pulled back to breathe, I gagged and drooled over his cock. I tried to wipe my mouth, but he caught my hand.

"Oh god, you've got me so close. You take my cock in your mouth so good. I could come down your throat right now," he groaned and sat up. He kissed me again, his breath shaking.

"Then do it," I taunted, my voice hoarse from the abuse my throat took.

He tilted his head to the side in challenge before knocking me onto my back. My head hit the pillow a split second before his mouth landed on my pussy. His breath still shook as he licked and sucked my responsive pussy. My body had been alert and buzzing with lust since we were making out. My moans came out desperate and wanton as he worked me over. His hands wrapped around my hips and his thumbs spread me open for him. He had me keening and coming in two minutes.

I was still in the throes of my orgasm when he jumped up and slammed into me. He slid in cleanly, and I was more than ready for it. "I don't know what takes my cock better, your pussy or your mouth," he said breathlessly over me.

Rolling my hips to match his thrusts, I tried to smile up at him. "You'll just have to test them more."

He moaned and leaned down to kiss my throat and a spot below my ear. The change in angle hitting the spot inside my body that made my legs go numb and come to pour out of me. My moan was more of a growl as I gripped him tightly around his back. The bed below me felt warm and wet and I could hear my come hitting his skin in a rhythmic pattern as he continued to fuck me.

"Yes, baby, come for me. Fucking soak it," he grunted. "Fucking soak that cock."

My vision blurred and my ears rang, but I was acutely aware of him chanting "Fuck, fuck, fuck," in my ear as he came with stuttering thrusts. Deep in his orgasm, he pushed into me further than before, rocking slightly, as he let his body take over. His hands shoved my hips onto his with enough force to leave handprints. A vein in his neck bulged with his pulse and I licked over it as it was all I could reach with his face still buried in my neck.

My body trembled with aftershocks as his body relaxed on top of mine. Eventually, he shifted so he was no longer crushing me. His eyes were closed in a relaxed doze. I was able to slip out to use the bathroom. I wandered naked for a moment before I found his bathroom. A soft knock sounded when I was washing my hands. "Hey, you okay?" Benjamin's voice sounded hesitant.

"Yeah, I was just going to the bathroom," I replied before I opened the door.

He was still naked like I was, and we both looked over each other's bodies. He smiled.

"Why?" I asked.

"I thought you were leaving or something," he explained as he crowded me into the bathroom.

"Why would I leave? We literally just said we'd co-own a store together," I said as I stepped backward in his small bathroom.

"I don't know. I just worried," he said and bent to kiss the top of my head before he stood in front of the toilet.

"Oh, I'm leaving now," I said and quickly left the bathroom as he started to pee.

His loud laugh followed me down the hall back to his kitchen, where I hunted for a glass for water. I was sipping it slowly, leaning against the counter and contemplating cleaning up the shattered glass from earlier, when he appeared in the doorway. He was wearing low slung black boxers and a white t-shirt.

"I left you some clothes on my bed," he said and came to take the glass of water out of my hand before finishing it.

"Thanks," I said, shyly now. I didn't know why, but I was feeling uncertain standing naked in Benjamin's kitchen after a round of great sex and our agreement. It didn't feel wrong or like I should leave. It felt more like I didn't know what to do next. In either our business agreement or our relationship.

There were so many risks attached to both, and to mix them together was likely a recipe for disaster. But nothing felt more right than our decision to work together and be together. I could practically hear my business professors screaming in horror from here.

I wordlessly left the kitchen to get dressed and met Benjamin in the living room. He had set out a pair of boxers and his larger version of the 2019 rib roast t-shirt for me to wear. He was sprawled out on the large couch under a fleece blanket with skulls and crossbones patterned on it. The edges were tied in that DIY way everyone was into a few years ago. He lifted the edge for me to climb in with him. The TV remote was in his hand, and he was scrolling Netflix.

"You're quiet," he said as I settled in as his little spoon. The hand holding the remote slung over my waist.

"I'm thinking," I said with a sigh.

"About what?" he asked, the unspoken "uh-oh" clear in his voice. He tossed the remote onto the coffee table.

"I'm worried we're signing ourselves up to get hurt," I said, and toyed with a knotted tassel of the blanket.

"Maybe," he sighed and stroked a hand up my arm. "But isn't everything in life a risk?"

"I guess," I admitted.

"Maybe sometimes we have to let go of control," he reasoned.

"Look at you and your personal growth," I deflected sarcastically.

He snorted a laugh. "I always knew giving up control was something I needed to do. I just wanted to make sure it was with the right person."

"And I'm that right person?" I asked and wiggled so I was facing him.

He looked thoughtful and pushed my hair away from my face. "I think so."

"Why?" I whispered.

"All the women I've been with before end up driving me nuts after a while. And you? You sure as hell drive me nuts, but I keep wanting more," he murmured, his eyes darting over my face and hair. Not nervously, but in a relaxed way, like he was taking all of me in. Cataloging me.

"Maybe you're just a masochist." I smiled.

He snorted a laugh again. "Maybe."

"What makes me different?" I asked, feeling self-conscious again.

He looked thoughtful again and waited a moment before answering. "Even when we were fighting over the store, you never told me to give up on my goals. You never told me my goals were stupid or not going to work. You never judged me for working at Oscar's. You never judged me for living in a townhouse and not working towards owning a home yet."

"Well, this is my first time here. That's bold of you to assume I wouldn't judge it," I reminded him.

He poked me in the ribs and rolled his eyes. "What do you think?" he asked and gestured around him.

"It's alright," I shrugged and then grinned.

"Hey, this is a brand new couch, and that is a huge TV," he said and pointed behind me.

"Oh, yes. All the important things," I joked.

"Anyway," he said, stretching out the syllables. "Other women I've been with have hated the Oscar's store events, the town events, and most of the people who live here. Sometimes they would think it was cute and quirky for a while but then they'd get bored. And, most of all, they didn't trust me. I could never feel truly settled with them because even when they agreed to let me control them in the bedroom, they weren't into it."

"They always held back; you mean?" I asked and toyed with a longer curl of his hair that had fallen over his forehead.

"We both were always wearing armor, if that makes sense. We were always faking something in the relationship," he said and closed his eyes while I played with his hair.

"I don't know if I can fake anything in a relationship," I said and watched as his curl sprung back as I let go of it.

He cracked open an eye as he smirked. "Yeah, I'd know if you were faking. I'd have less laundry to do."

"Stop," I laughed and smacked his pec. "It doesn't always happen. But really, I meant I don't think I have the emotional energy to fake anything in a relationship. I don't have the time to stay in a relationship that equals a net zero gain. That's not to say I won't put in work, I will, but a relationship can't always be more work than what I receive out of it."

"What a businesswoman," Benjamin laughed.

"I know, it sounds harsh," I said with a shake of my head. "But I've had really shitty relationships in the past and I've learned from them."

"I didn't say it was harsh," he said. "But now I know you'll be the one handling our business expenses."

I laughed too. "So, what is our store called?"

"Books and Tramp Stamps?" he suggested. His lips curled up at the corners.

"Tats and Texts?" I suggested.

"Symbolism," he listed.

"Hm, I like that. It's related to both. But maybe too long for a single word store name," I considered and settled further into the couch against him.

"Symbols," he amended.

"Eh, sounds like a music shop," I dismissed.

"Cymbal and symbol are totally different words," he said, correcting me. He sounded much too excited to correct me on something.

"No, I know," I assured him, and he deflated. "But they sound too similar."

"Inks," he suggested.

"Wait. Ink," I said and looked up at him.

We stared at each other for a moment and then broke out in grins.

"Yes," he said. "Ink."

I kicked my feet excitedly and squealed and he reached over to the coffee table for his phone.

"What are you doing?" I asked him.

"I'm calling my realtor. We can go through yours. Mine's a total dick," he said as he selected the contact.

I was in a focused state as I jumped up for my phone and jotted down a few notes in the notes app. I heard him fire his realtor and tell him to rescind his offer on the store.

"Hey, what is your loan for?" I asked him as I returned from my phone call to Susan. She was thrilled my only competition for the store was backing out. But mostly she was excited to be the first to know the small-town gossip that was me and Benjamin.

Benjamin leaned over the cleaned kitchen table and looked at some paperwork. He handed me his loan approval paperwork. It was considerably more than mine and signed by Donnie.

"What the hell? Why is yours so much higher than mine?" I shouted.

"Because I'm a man, baby, yeah," he said, quoting Austin Powers.

I rolled my eyes and looked at his paperwork. It was his

sketches of the store layout and the plans he had for owning the space himself.

"You know, I still don't know if you're even a good tattooist," I said.

He swung around. "I showed you pictures," he defended.

"Yeah, but the one on your arm..." I said, knowing I was poking the bear that was his artistic pride.

"That's not fair! That's like saying you couldn't know good books since you've read... you've read... what's a romance book people judge each other for reading?" He struggled.

"*Twilight... Fifty Shades of Grey*," I said with a shrug.

"Yeah, those," he said and crossed his arms over his chest.

"Those books served their purposes and I respect them," I said. "*Twilight* gave a bunch of millennial young adults a clean romance with enough escapism to take their minds off the trauma that was their adolescence being torn apart and dissected and judged by news media around the clock. And *Fifty Shades* introduced kink to millions of stagnant marriages at the tail end of the 2008 financial crisis."

"Okay, okay," he submitted with an annoyed shake of his head.

"Show me how good you are at tattooing," I demanded.

He unfolded his arms to grab for his phone.

"No, I want you to tattoo me," I said, getting to the reason I baited him to begin with.

"No," he replied.

"Yes."

"No, Layla," he said and practically stomped his foot like a child. "I don't tattoo-"

"Girlfriends," I finished for him. "I know, and I'm not your girlfriend."

He looked crestfallen. "Then what are you?"

"You haven't asked me yet. Ask me after," I said with a grin.

His face brightened, and he shook his head in disbelief.

"I'm good at finding loopholes in the fine print," I explained.

"Should have known," he challenged.

"I excelled in Business Law 101," I expanded.

He rolled his eyes again. I was beginning to like the sight of his eyes rolled back in his head. It tended to mean I was winning. The argument or an orgasm.

"Fine," he huffed out.

I beamed.

"What do you want and where?" he asked in a tone befitting Eeyore.

"You choose," I said as he started walking towards his bedroom.

"What?!" he whirled back to me. "You're begging me for a tattoo, and you don't even know what you want?"

"Nope, I trust you to choose."

He let out a growl of frustration and opened the door to another room. It was a second bedroom turned into a mini tattoo station.

He slammed open a box of his tools and nodded for me to sit on the chair. I gleefully hopped up.

"I'm giving you a tattoo of Oscar's store logo on your ass," he growled, irritated.

"No, thank you," I said innocently.

"Thigh, okay? I really like thigh pieces on girls," he mumbled as he opened up a razor package.

"Yes," I agreed, and pulled the boxers up over my right thigh.

He was silent as he shaved my thigh and cleaned the area. I leaned back in the vinyl chair and watched.

"Do you tattoo many people here?" I asked.

"Shut up, I'm concentrating," he grunted back at me.

I smiled and watched through hooded eyes. From start to finish, it took less than an hour. He only looked up at me after he did the first quick line. One brow raised.

"Oh, uh, green," I said.

He scoffed and went back to work.

Did it hurt? Yeah, a little. But nothing like I was led to believe it would as a child. I settled back and watched his face as he worked, choosing not to look at the tattoo. When he tattooed, he wore glasses. As he slid them on his face, a pink blush was present like he was waiting for me to comment on them. But I would not make fun of him for glasses when he was literally making permanent marks on my skin. I watched as his tongue peeked out between his lips as he drew on my skin, and I found it endearing. His brow was furrowed in concentration and his brown eyes intense on my skin and his work.

The pain was consistent throughout the procedure and fell into white noise with the buzzing of the gun. I was dozing lightly, listening to the gun and the crickets outside, when he sat back. His back cracked along his spine as he stretched out his muscles.

"There, I'm d- of fucking course you're asleep," he swore.

"I'm not," I said drowsily.

He looked me over with an eyebrow raised and cocked his head with a sigh, like he just realized what he was getting himself into. I wasn't sure what that meant.

I looked down at my thigh and saw a simple black lined open book. One page had an apple and the other page had a knife. To anyone else, this would look like a weird choice for a tattoo, but to me and Benjamin, it was a picture of our beginning. And it certainly wasn't the logo for Oscar's store.

"I love it," I whispered.

"Will you be my girlfriend now?" he asked harshly, like I had bullied him into waiting.

"Do a second one and I'll con-"

"Layla!"

"Fine, yes. I'll be your girlfriend," I laughed.

"Good, get back in the bed while I clean up," he said. I slid off the vinyl chair, my skin skidding as I went.

He snapped the gloves he had just taken off at my ass as I walked away, smiling and giggling.

We had sex again when he came back in, careful to avoid the plastic wrapped area on my thigh that had admittedly begun to ache. We stayed up all night planning our store. The layout, the design, the logo, the events, and the parties. We agreed Oscar and Donna got free tattoos and books for life, as they were both integral to our store's existence. I even pulled up the website of the business furniture company for us to pick out what we thought would work best. It was exhilarating and validating to work with someone on a common goal. Even more exciting to think that this was Benjamin- who, until maybe six months ago, was just my hot manager that I barely spoke to. And now I knew intimately the face he made when he came while I rode him.

20

It was barely nine in the morning when Susan called me. Benjamin and I were asleep on his bed amongst scribbled plans and notes and rumpled bed sheets. At about three in the morning, we had stopped our planning to have some freezer pizza and wine but ended up falling asleep instead of working more.

"Hello?" I answered the phone in a panic. It wasn't often I got a call in the morning that woke me up.

"Layla, it's Susan. You've got it. The Schmidts accepted your first offer. You've got the store," came Susan's no-nonsense voice.

"Really?" I said excitedly and sat up. I slapped Benjamin's back to wake him up.

He jumped awake and grabbed my leg like he was making sure I was okay. I patted his hand and listened to Susan give me the next steps that Benjamin and I had to do to make the sale final. When I hung up after setting a meeting for later this afternoon, Benjamin was wide awake and writing everything he had overheard.

"It's real," I said to him as I threw my phone down.

"It's real," he echoed with finality and sat down on the bed in front of me.

"You're real," I said quieter now.

He considered me warmly for a moment. "You're real... real smelly."

I threw a pillow at him. He caught it easily with a grin. "We ate garlicky pizza and drank wine before falling asleep! I haven't brushed my teeth yet."

He was chuckling as he got up to get dressed. "Well, let's get cleaned up and we can swing by your place before we go stop at Oscar's."

Benjamin dressed in a pair of dark wash but worn jeans, a white undershirt, and a blue flannel. I watched as he dressed, as mesmerized by the slow covering of his beautiful body as I was by his undressing. He knew I was watching, and he stopped to flex a few times, a silly smile on his face. It reminded me of the time after our date when he had watched me change.

"I knew you were there," I whispered with a blush.

He looked at me, his head tilted like a confused puppy.

"After our date. In Oscar's office," I continued in a whisper.

I watched as red splotches of a blush appeared across his neck and cheeks.

"Hm," he said brightly as he turned away from me to select a simple knotted silver chain necklace from the top of his cluttered dresser. "Knives, blood, exhibitionism, voyeurism, light bondage... is there anything else I should know?"

I giggled. "I'll let you know when I read something else intriguing."

He shook his head and looked at me as he clasped the chain behind his neck. "It's always the quiet bookworms, isn't it?"

"Oh, yes," I agreed.

Oscar was thrilled for our news of opening a store together. Tears had dripped into his mustache, and they rolled off the ends, making it look like his mustache was also crying. Benjamin and I decided later that it wasn't an impossibility. Oscar had decided to make it an event, and on Friday evening, the store closed for our last day with a pizza party. Joe's Place delivered sheets of pizza (Joe's Place being actually called Romano's Italiano, Romano being the surname of Joe's family that had owned the place for decades, but affectionately called Joe's Place by the entire town), Scoot of Scoot's Bar delivered tons of beer and wine (actually called Corner Bar and Inn, but no inn has existed there in probably thirty years), and the Edible Entertainment girls brought their sound system (and wearing casual clothes this time). Though, most importantly, Donna brought many trays of her peanut butter bars.

The party began with Oscar ceremoniously placing a Help Wanted sign on the door. It read:

Help Wanted
Benjamin and Layla's shifts
NO OVERNIGHTS

Seeing the sign being placed on the window brought a lump of tears to my throat. Oscar's store had been my first job as an emancipated teen. And had continued as my only job. It paid for my college education, my apartment, my car, my books, and was the only family I had ever known. I wasn't really leaving the place. Benjamin and I had already agreed to take part in events and come to all the parties. Oscar was the only grocer in town and was directly next door to our new store. We'd still see them every day. But the finality of that sign. It hit me then- like little things had been hitting me since we decided to open our store together. It struck me deep in my guts and felt like grief. I knew Benjamin felt similarly, but he kept his cool better than I did.

Oscar hugged me tightly right after the sign went up. His sobs and mine shook us until Benjamin helped pry Oscar off of me. "I'm so proud of you," Oscar had sobbed, his mustache drooping with moisture. "My little Layla is all grown up."

Donna scoffed through misty eyes next to us. "Alright, alright," she said in her rasping smoker's voice. "It's not like she's your kid or anything."

"Oh wait," Benjamin said with twinkling eyes. "You mean you and Oscar aren't her parents? I've worked here for over five years, and I thought you two were her parents."

He was joking, but it broke the dam that held back Donna's tears. She gave him a furious glare and then stomped off.

I spent the rest of the evening eating pizza, dancing with the girls from Edible Entertainment, dancing with Benjamin, and talking with the partygoers. Greg handed us a binder of information about the care and maintenance of the image of our storefronts to maintain the historical nature of it. It was much like a homeowner's association, but much less official and more of Greg's personal tastes. Scoot grumbled something at us about offering him discounts on coffee if he offered us discounts on draft beers. We agreed as long as he also threw in a bowl of his beef stew.

Benjamin and I hadn't been near each other much during the

party and had behaved rather conservatively when we were both in the same conversations. It hadn't occurred to us that nobody knew about the change in our relationship status until they saw us kiss. We stopped dancing for a drink break and stood in the small line in front of the beer cooler, holding hands. I looked up at him with a smile. Sweat beaded on both of our foreheads from the efforts of dancing, and he smiled down at me. It felt natural for him to lean down and kiss me. A gasp went up around us and Benjamin's lips froze on mine.

"Uh oh," he mumbled against my lips, and I couldn't help the laugh that bubbled out.

"I knew it!" Donna was shouting triumphantly.

"Oh, my *babies*!" Oscar was drunkenly shouting, raising his beer to us.

"Wait, nobody knew?" Anna, of Edible Entertainment, asked. She turned to laugh with Betsy and Lily. "They've been together for ages!"

"Actually," Benjamin said, his blush ferociously staining his cheeks. "It's pretty new."

"The parade?" Lily asked, laughing and clutching Anna.

I shook my head, biting my lip. The party had all but stopped around us.

"You treat her right," Oscar said, approaching us now. His mustache was stiff over his lip. "I don't want to hear about you hurting her."

Benjamin pinched me just above my elbow and all I could think of was the healing B carved into my skin. I snorted. "He wouldn't dare," I told Oscar assuredly. It was probably the wine talking, but I decided, at that moment, that when Benjamin and

I got married, Oscar would walk me down the aisle. And Donna would be my flower girl.

It was only a few days later that Benjamin and I picked up the keys to the store. We had packed my car full of cleaning supplies and snacks and were ready for a day of cleaning. It was bitterly cold out, now closer to winter than it was autumn. We stood outside the store; the key clutched in Benjamin's hand.

"This is it," he said slowly.

"Yes, please open the door. It's freezing out here," I said through chattering teeth.

"Wow, okay, I was trying to take in this special moment," he scoffed and then unlocked the glass doors.

Just before I pushed in, he grabbed me about the waist and hoisted me into the air. I didn't understand what he was doing, so I thrashed around for a second. I ended up slung over his shoulder like a sack of grain. "Fucking hell, Layla," he laughed as he opened the door. "I was trying to carry you over the threshold and be all romantic and shit. But I guess this works, too."

I strained to look behind me as he entered the store and the door closed softly after us. It was dusty and there were scuffs on the wood floor from where the wax had been worn away. A few bits of paper and fabric samples were strewn about. But it was perfect. It was ours.

Benjamin set me down as we both silently looked around. It was quiet, only the low hum of the heating and a car going by on the cobblestone street. "Wow," he said quietly and spun slowly in a circle.

"Wow," I parroted back to him in agreement.

"Wait," he said and then lifted me again, this time bridal

style. I was giggling as he walked us to the back rooms. There was a restroom, a storage closet, and an office that still had an antique desk and chairs. Benjamin set me on the desk gently and smirked mischievously at me. "We need to christen the store."

"Now?" I asked, even though I was reaching for his fly.

"Hell yeah, little one," he chuckled and lifted my shirt over my head.

I shoved his pants down over his ass and thighs, followed by his boxers. He reached into the pocket of his leather jacket and pulled out the soft rope we had used in the bedroom a few times now. "Lay back," he demanded after undressing me.

I obeyed and waited as he tied my arms and legs to each leg of the desk. The surface of the desk was cold against my skin, but seemed clean. Benjamin stood next to the desk wearing only his leather jacket now. He had put it back on after I had eyed it on the chair. It hung open on his muscled and tattooed chest. My mouth watered. He grinned at me menacingly as he flicked open his pocket knife. I shivered.

"It's quiet here," he said simply as he traced the knife over my breasts. The tip of the knife left a slight scratch on my skin. No blood was drawn, but I could see the red welt rising around my breasts. My breath heaved in my chest as he trailed the knife down over my stomach. "So quiet. And we're the only ones with the keys."

He traced the scratching knife over and around my navel. I shivered.

"Is this blade warm or cold?" he asked me. His voice was steady but casual, like he was discussing anything other than the knife against my skin. When he spoke in that casual, easy way with a knife to me, it made me more on edge. It seemed like he wasn't taking what he was doing seriously. But I knew otherwise. I knew he was hyper focused on me and my reactions.

I closed my eyes as he dipped the knife lower. "It's... cold, no, it's hot. I can't tell." The scratch he left behind burned, and I thought maybe he had actually cut me. I couldn't lift my head enough to see. He tilted the knife so the broad, flat side rested against my lower stomach. "It's the same temperature as my skin."

He picked the knife up and blew a hot, long breath over it before returning it to my skin. I knew it was only slightly warmer, if at all, but my over sensitive skin seemed like it burned at the touch of the knife. I hissed in a breath.

"Open your eyes," he breathed.

I obeyed.

"I want you to keep your eyes on me," he said as he trailed the knife over my mound and then over my thigh that didn't have a healing tattoo on it. The knife scratched as it went. He bent over me and licked my skin, following the red scratching line over my breasts, my stomach, my mound, and then down to my thigh. The soothing, searing, wet touch of his tongue had me panting and straining against the ropes. When the trail of scratches ended at my thigh, his breath ghosted over my pussy. He breathed on me while I anticipated his next move. The heat of his breath puffed over my pussy for so long that I thought he would not touch me. I strained and whined in the ropes. My skin was so sensitive that even his breath felt like touch and I felt my arousal drip down to the desk.

"Benjamin," I pleaded, keeping my eyes on him. He was alternating between watching my face and my dripping pussy.

He gave a quick lick over my wetness, and I practically screamed. He chuckled darkly before doing it again. I swore he could have done it one more time and I would have come right there. He gently blew cold air over my heated skin, and I shivered. He licked a slow, hot line up the center of my core and I bit my lip to keep from screaming now. My legs trembled in their restraints, but I didn't take my eyes from Benjamin. He licked me again before closing his lips around my clit gently and sucking. I was just about to come when he ran the knife over my hip bone. It felt like he had sliced me and my body shrank away from the metal blade as much as I could. He switched hands with the knife and brought me to the edge once again and sliced at the other hip bone. I didn't see any blood well up at the cuts, so I knew there was no cut but it felt like he had carved into me. My body was so sensitive that just a touch felt like a cut.

I was begging and pleading with him now, and he stood up. He walked around the desk to where my head was and forcibly tilted my head back. He shoved his cock deep into my mouth. I gagged around him, my eyes watering, before he pulled out. He gave me a moment to breathe and then pushed back in.

"Good girl, take my fucking cock. I love your lips stretching around me. So fucking hot. Yeah, let me see you lick it. Flick the head with your tongue- oh *fuck* yes. How deep can I go? How deep? Let me see you- shit, yeah, that's my good girl." He fucked my mouth until his abs were quivering with the urge to fuck into me and come. My mascara had run down my face and into my hair at my temples and tears flowed as he gagged me repeatedly.

He pulled out of my mouth sharply and walked around to lean on the desk again to lick me more.

"Let me get another taste of this pussy. This sweet pussy," he groaned. This time I was shivering with anticipation, my core clenching with need. I loved when he lost himself in fucking me. Or, rather, lost his sensibilities and became his most animalistic self.

He inserted a finger. And then a second one, gathering my wetness while he licked and sucked at my clit. It didn't take long with his curling fingers and sucking at my clit to have me coming. "Come for me. Let me see how hard you can come. Don't hold back, I wanna see it. I wanna taste it. Yeah, fucking give it to me."

The knife had been dropped when he was fucking my mouth and all the orgasm denials had heightened this one. I looked down at him and saw his smiling face, eyes closed, still sucking on my clit. He was vigorously fucking me with his fingers, and I was coming so hard it splashed over the desk and his chest. He had removed the leather jacket at some point, I noticed, and I soaked his skin with my release. I vaguely heard my squealing voice through the explosion in my mind that was my orgasm.

When my orgasm faded slightly, he pulled away and hopped up onto the desk and sunk into me for a moment before he pulled out, swearing. He quickly pulled the loose ropes on my wrists and ankles to untie them and flipped me over. I was on elbows and knees on our new wooden desk in a puddle of my own come as he got back up behind me.

He sunk into me with a low groan, and I breathed through the sensation of the new angle. He moaned, "This is what I wanted, fucking beautiful." I was already dripping around his cock as he pumped in and out of me. I couldn't help it once he had me started. He gripped my hips hard enough to bruise and slammed into me a few times before slowing. He alternated between hard and fast and slow, tilting thrusts. His grunting and moaning had me wanting to stay there all day. He was so vocal during sex, and I loved it.

I realized I was begging him over and over to "Fuck me, fuck me, fuck me." I bit my lip. He realized I was trying to stifle my moans, and he bent over and reached and hand up to my face. He shoved two fingers deep into my mouth and fucked me while I gagged and sucked on his fingers. His thrusts took on more of a scooping motion, and I knew he was just about to come. I pushed back in time with his thrusts and met him halfway with a wet slapping sound. I was close to coming again, and I held on, hoping we'd come at the same time.

His moans became more guttural as he fucked me with an upward tipping thrust, and his breathing was ragged and desperate. My nails curled on the edge of the desk as I erupted for the second time. I looked down to see my release dripping down Benjamin's thighs and hitting the desk below me. My muscles gave out, and I collapsed on the desk. Benjamin growled and flipped me over onto my back. He fisted his cock twice before he came, head tilted back and chest heaving, all over my stomach and chest. He came so hard it coated my chest and neck, a rope of it landing on my lips and cheek.

He looked down at me with a lopsided, lazy and satiated grin. His blonde curls falling over his forehead. "You need a shower," he said hoarsely.

I licked over my lips slowly, gathering the come that had landed there. His eyes zeroed in on my tongue as it gathered up his come. I swallowed it down and smiled up at him sweetly. "And whose fault is that?"

"Mine," he said. "All mine."

21

Epilogue

Opening day for Ink was halfway into February. Streamers and balloons decorated the store, and a big red ribbon was waiting to be cut outside the front doors. Benjamin and I stood just inside our store with Oscar and Donna. Donna had just finished helping me straighten up the bookshelves and put out the last box of books. Oscar had given Benjamin a pep talk about owning a business while Benjamin wiped down his tattoo chair one more time. We met in the middle of the store while our town's Mayor spoke to a few reporters and a small crowd of our neighbors about how excited he was to have a new business in the area. I took a deep, steadying breath of the smell of vanilla, coffee, eucalyptus, and books. I gripped Benjamin's hand and Donna rubbed my back soothingly.

"Here we go," Benjamin said quietly as we approached the doors. Oscar and Donna held the double doors open while Benjamin and I stepped out to the ribbon.

There was a polite but excited round of applause as the mayor handed us the ceremonial large scissors. I looked around and saw the entire staff from Oscar's store, Greg, the Schmidts, Scoot, the librarians, and an acceptable amount of people from town. Everyone was smiling and looked eager to come into our store.

Benjamin and I both gripped the large scissors in our hands and posed for the local reporters. I smiled brightly for the picture, fighting back tears at how accomplished I felt.

I had worked hard for this. I had put myself through college, saved up for a store, gotten a loan, and bought this place. Benjamin had met me where I had needed him, and I did the same for him. Our ideas could be entwined with little compromise to our original independent goals. It felt right and true to myself to find someone whose path was so aligned with my own.

I had moved in with Benjamin not long after we bought the store. It helped with costs and my lease was up before his. Now that our incomes were nonexistent until the store had been open for a few months, we had to be more mindful. Truthfully, I didn't mind moving in with Benjamin so soon after beginning our relationship. We quickly fell into a comfortable rhythm working together and living together.

A lot of time had been spent cleaning and repairing the building as the Schmidt's ability to maintain the property had waned as they aged. The floors needed a good buff and a thick coat of wax, the brick walls needed to be cleaned, and the drywall needed patched and painted. The bathrooms had been gutted and remodeled, the storage closet was ripped apart and put back together cleanly, and the office was painted and decorated. And that was all before we had the delivery of the long pastry case and put in the café plumbing and counters and appliances, the bookshelves, the till, and the tattoo equipment. It had been months of hard work, often around the clock. And now we were here, ready to have our first customers through the doors.

The little crowd counted down and Benjamin and I cut the ribbon with a flourish. The crowd cheered and cameras flashed. Later, I would see the picture chosen for the paper and call the newspaper to have it printed and framed for me. I was beaming at the camera, Benjamin had a proud arm around my shoulders and a bright blush on his cheeks as he grinned at the photographer, and Oscar and Donna were behind us, holding the doors, and looking like proud parents. I hung the picture next to the one Benjamin had taken on our first date.

Half of the crowd went in to the left where my carefully curated and lovingly placed book shelves were piled high and ready to be perused. Half of the crowd went to the right where artfully framed pictures of Benjamin's previous tattoo art was featured as well as his pricing. Benjamin and I stood in the middle, smiling and watching, until Donna yelled for us. "Hey, lovebirds! I don't work for you! Why am I working your till?"

I laughed and Benjamin ran to the till while I ran to the café, where I would make lattes and cappuccinos as fast as I could for hours until the crowd cleared out for the evening. Benjamin had kept his schedule book at the till with him and he had booked himself solid for two months. I had sold a quarter of the books I had out on the shelves and Benjamin had kept a list of books for me to order and names and numbers of waiting customers.

I locked the door after our last customer and turned to Benjamin. He was leaning over the counter like he couldn't stand up anymore. "We need to put a bed in the back. I can't make it home," he wailed dramatically.

He sprawled over the couch we had set up by the windows and looked over his schedule while I closed the till and turned off the big gold chandeliers. We were still silent, all talked out and hoarse after our busy day, as we made our way to Benjamin's car in the big lot. Benjamin and I stopped short when we saw a car parked in the lot and I sniffled back tears. Waiting in his car with three corgis was a sleepy-looking Oscar. There was Oscar, waiting to see us leave our store after our first day as shop owners. He was camped out with his dogs, just like our first overnight shift at his store. He was smiling at us and his corgis went wild in the back seat when they saw us.

Benjamin cleared his throat twice, like he was trying to clear a lump from this throat. "Oscar," he tried to say in a stern tone, but it quivered with emotion. "Go home!"

About the Author

Cat Austen is a romance author based in Ohio. She lives with her husband and their two boys. She enjoys gardening and baking and is a voracious reader of romance novels.

Connect with her on TikTok, Instagram, and Facebook
@CatAustenAuthor
Subscribe to her newsletter at cataust024.com/subscribe